LAST TESTAMENT
OF
CRIGHTON
SMYTHE

GAVIN GARDINER

Content compiled for publication by Richard Mayers
of *Burton Mayers Books*.
Cover design by ebooklaunch.com

First published by Burton Mayers Books 2021.
All rights reserved.

A CIP catalogue record for this book is available from
the British Library

ISBN: 1-8384845-5-2
ISBN-13: 978-1-8384845-5-2

Typeset in **Adobe Garamond**

www.BurtonMayersBooks.com

To those who so relentlessly support me in my pursuit
of the nightmares of my mind, I salute you.

Heather, Dad, Jamie, Hannah, John, Kyle, Derek, Rayner,
Liliana, Miguel, Alana, Sibby, Miriam, Lari, Elliot, Becky,
Tori, and everyone in between, I thank you all.

A special thanks goes out to Craig and the team at Close to
the Bone Publications for taking a chance on this tale in
the first instance, and helping make Crighton what he is
before his eventual emigration over to his current home at
Burton Mayers Books. Crighton and myself owe a
tremendous amount to the talented, dedicated,
and patient professionals in both camps, and we
offer our unending gratitude.

And Mum: you've spent hours, days, weeks, and endless
phone calls meticulously trawling through every word I've
ever written. Amongst much else, thanks for always egging
me on to ramp up the gore. Crighton's your
baby as much as mine, I'm afraid.

A brutal and distressing strain of horror has been poured into the pages of this novella. Anyone reading should take a moment to consider whether this is a depth into which they should dive.

I believe it is.

I remember waiting for Mr. Rivera, who will die from a brain hemorrhage fourteen years and seven months from now, to return to his office so I could sneak out of Pleasance Heights. How odd to know the exact time and manner of everyone's death but your own. Didn't see mine coming and now here I am.

My name is Crighton Smythe, and this is the story of how I died.

Might as well start with Baby Buggy Lady. So I've left our apartment building and there I am, making my way down Delphi Street, trudging through the snow. It's hard not to bash into people when you have your earplugs in and you're looking up at the rooftops. See, I had this knack where I could see in folks' faces exactly how and when they were going to die. It worked with hearing just a voice most times, too. Sometimes I felt like my brain was going to explode with all the death, so I wore the earplugs and kept my eyes to the rooftops as a way to dull the knack. I liked rooftops, so it was okay. You could get out onto the roof of our apartment then all the way down our street and round onto Jocasta Avenue if you followed the buildings. Livvy and I used to sit out on our roof all the time. Before we died, that is.

So it's pretty cold with all the snow, but I'm wearing the parka, gloves, and hat that Livvy – crappers, sorry, that's my ma – gave me for our nights on the roof. Anyways, I've come out here to do something so I better get it done. I take a big bite of butter, pop the plugs out of my ears, and lower my eyes to the streets. The sound of the

1

city rushes in. Some guy (*Cardiovascular disease, fifty-third birthday!*) is standing on a crate barking through a megaphone about all that crummy 'Nam business. There's always someone yacking on about that these days. I got enough death buzzing round my head without having to hear that. But that's when I see Baby Buggy Lady, entering stage left out of some department store. Nearly walk right into her but I'm pretty quick on my feet, despite my size, so I skip a step to avoid her then stand aside and let her pass. I wince as the usual earache throbs in the sides of my head, but I manage to turn the grimace into a big goofy grin, spread right across my face for Baby Buggy Lady. Her eyebrows arch warily. She smiles back.

Then I see it.

Garbage truck, twenty minutes!

Or bus. Or something. I wasn't sure at that moment to be honest, but I knew it was big, and I knew it was soon. Didn't much like the thought of seeing someone die, but this knack of mine was getting so intense I had to see if there was any truth to it. This was just what I'd been traipsing around looking for: someone on their way out soon whose death I could see for myself. If I was right, Baby Buggy Lady's time was only minutes away.

So I follow her, keeping my distance. Besides my boots in the snow I don't make a sound. Never have. Livvy always said I was quiet as a fox. But yeah, I pick up my pace to match the woman's. Getting a bit nervous I'll have one of my stupid lousy blackouts before I get to see what I need to see, but I'm feeling all right. I'm taking another bite of butter from the block in my parka pocket (starting to melt) when Baby Buggy Lady suddenly disappears round a corner. I hurry. Not that I need to. There was still another few streets before the life was demolished from her and her baby.

Then I hear it, the bellowing of the eighteen-wheeler. I start to feel dizzy, as anyone would gearing up to see something like this. *Don't black out*, I keep telling myself. *Don't black out, don't black out, don't black out.*

So I keep to the shadows while I wait for the inevitable. Baby Buggy Lady must be deaf, dumb, and blind to step in front of the semi, but she does. I must sound like a piece of work to you, but she had it coming. I'm telling you, everyone in this city's the same. Anyways, it's all too fast for me to make out much detail, but I do see Baby Buggy Lady's baby buggy fold in on itself in much the same way as they get folded up on the bus. Can't say the woman folds up quite as neat; her whole body kind of wraps around the front of the truck, the way a water balloon might hug around a baseball bat before it explodes. Jeez, I dunno. It was over so quick. All that mattered was that the vision had come true.

The death I saw in people's faces and heard in their voices, it was real.

***

Right, so I've seen Baby Buggy Lady and Baby Buggy Baby smash into a zillion pieces. Livvy – remember, that's my ma – doesn't like me leaving the apartment on account of my blackouts, so I head home quick before she gets back from work. Another reason she doesn't like me leaving is that I have a bit of black in me from Pa, and she doesn't want me going the way he went. People don't always like 'half-casts' like me, or even blacks – Pa's death made that clear. I know she'd like to move us to Bordeaux where she grew up ('France is so *safe* and the French are so *gracious*,' she likes to remind me) but we just don't have the money for moves. Instead, she pulled me right out of school when he died and told me I was best staying in the apartment. Talk about paranoid. So I've been practically locked up these past years, but I started to wonder more and more if my knack was real. Wouldn't you? It's not nice, having visions of death shoved in your face like that, but I had to get out and see if there was any truth to it, and Baby Buggy Lady was enough to convince me there was. So yeah, Livvy preferred me to stay in and write. I was a playwright, you see. Well, I hoped to be. But we'll get back to that.

After the mom and baby thing I chuck my butter (gone slimy; hate it when it's slimy) and head back to our apartment building. I'm stepping into the lobby of Pleasance Heights – that makes it sound like a fancy hotel, but it's actually a dive – and I hear Livvy tearing up hell on the landing. She's running door to door, screaming her darned head off looking for me. I follow the sound of the commotion. She spots me. Runs straight at me like a heat-seeking missile. I look down and see dots of blood speckling the arm of her blouse.

'What did you do to yourself, Livvy?' I ask her, genuinely shocked but pretending I don't already know about the cutting, a habit I thought she was finally done with. She grabs me by the shoulders with a strength that contradicts her size.

'Why did you leave the apartment, Crighton?' she squawks. 'Why, *why*, WHY?'

I'm trying to play it cool, as I do around Livvy, but she's shaking me and shouting and going a bit nuts. I always get a bit nervous when she gets herself worked up, on the grounds of the episodes she used to have when she was a girl. Oh, sorry. We'll get to that, too. Anyways, things have been weird with her lately, and we've not been quite as close as usual, so I'm a little on edge. Luckily she calms down, then leads me along the landing to our apartment. In we go, but there's another scare on the cards for poor old Crighton.

Stacks of flattened cardboard boxes. Everywhere.

'Son, I'm sorry I've been so distant with you,' says Livvy, the usual gentle strain returning to her voice. The remnants of her French accent slip through, such serene inflections. Music to my ears. 'It's just we've been a bit behind on the rent. Mr. Rivera has bills to pay, too. I've told you how important it is to pay what you owe.'

Yeah, yeah. Rent can't go unpaid. Taxes help those less fortunate, give them something when they're down on their luck. Heard it all before. Livvy's the smartest person I know, and I get the rent part, but the rest is such garbage. She spends her life running around town caring for all the old crones – crones that are just older versions of the scum on the streets. There's a plague out there, a plague of criminals, rapists, and vermin. That's it, *vermin*. Have to remember that one. Anyways, we don't owe them nothing, that's for sure. But I smile and nod and play it cool. She's still the best person I know. How could she be anything else?

'I understand. But you're sure you're all right, Livvy?' I glance again at the dots of blood on her sleeve.

'*Oui, mon chéri,*' she says lightly, putting her hands behind her back. 'But Crighton, you know I prefer you calling me Mom.'

'Okay, Mom.'

A pause lingers in the air, a tiny vacuum waiting to be filled with more bad news.

'My love, he's asked us to leave.'

So here I am, standing amongst all these boxes, being told we're out. What's going to happen? Won't have my ma sleeping in one of those shelters with the – what was it? – *vermin*. Where'll we go? What'll we do? My head's spinning. Can't take all the uncertainty, all the questions. Feel like a blackout's on the way, until I suddenly remember what I know.

I look deep into Livvy's delicate face, past her make-up that's all smeared and blotched from her crying and carrying on. Deeper than anyone can look into any face.

And there it is.

She's lying on a sprawling super queen size bed back in Bordeaux. Queen size for a queen. Her dying seconds are playing out right in front of me. She's surrounded by warm faces smiling down at her, those of the family I'll come to raise. The glowing faces are all right there with her in these final moments, but it's my face she's looking up at. In her eyes: gratitude. I see it clear as can be, how grateful she is for all I've given her. See, my playwriting is going to make us rich. Big house, big family, and a peaceful death for my sweet Livvy in unlimited comfort. No more pain, and certainly no more cutting.

So you see, I know everything's going to be okay. I've seen it.

At least I thought I had.

Livvy's looking at me like she's seen it too. Finally I see that smile, the one missing these past few weeks. You haven't met her so you don't know, but that smile is like nothing you've ever seen.

Anyways, her anger at my leaving the apartment has fizzled out. Even though our home's being taken from us, the future I see in her eyes reminds me that all we need is each other. I hated my knack when I was alive – it was a curse, really – but at the time I was grateful it had shown me how she was going to pass. Nothing else mattered other than getting to where I knew we were headed. She pulls a pine cone from her coat and places it in my hand, pressing my fingers around it. Always did love pine cones, my Livvy.

Suddenly, from the open door, the sound of a man clearing his throat.

'Mr. Rivera,' says Livvy, 'Crighton and I were just about to start packing. I wanted to ask you how long we have to—'

'Please, Olivia,' he interrupts, those beady eyes locked on her, 'no more "Mr. Rivera". Call me Art.'

This is the Hispanic guy that owns the building. Lives down the hall with his old ma. The smell of burritos or enchiladas or some other Mexican food from their apartment always makes my stomach rumble. Loves to cook, loves Christmas, and loves to make my blood boil.

Always starts wearing his lousy Christmas sweaters months too early, so there it is, a goddamn Christmas tree standing right in our front door that's no longer our front door. As if there wasn't already enough Christmas everywhere. Seems like the kindest man you've ever met at first, but he's not. He's stroking that creepy goatee and staring right into my Livvy's eyes. She looks down at the floor like a shy schoolgirl, and in that moment he catches my gaze over her shoulder and mouths the word, *that* word. The same word he always mouths in my direction.

Leech.

I tighten my trembling fist. I feel the blood rush to my face.

Brain hemorrhage, brain hemorrhage, brain hemorrhage,

I keep reminding myself. *Just you wait. Brain hemorrhage's on its way. Only fourteen years and seven months to go, you crummy old bonehead.*

'Olivia, you and Crighton have always been such pleasant tenants to have in the building. *Pleasant* tenants... Just what we need in Pleasance Heights!' His shoulders bounce as he guffaws at what I surmise to be his idea of a joke. Livvy giggles, keeping up the schoolgirl act. 'Reliability: that's the only issue. But I've been wondering if that really must spell the end of your residency.' (Yeah, the creep really does talk like that.) 'After all, it *is* Christmas.'

And so what followed was their first stroll down the landing together, the start of their little 'arrangement'. Don't get the wrong idea about Livvy; my ma would never have done anything like this unless she absolutely had to, and I guess she must have felt she did. She believed in my playwriting, and that when I finally hammered out the play to end all plays everything would change for us. She just figured this was one more thing she had to do in the meantime.

So there they go, Mr. Rivera leading her down the hall, exiting stage right into an empty apartment. Once he's closed the door, I slip down the landing and stand outside to try and hear what they're talking about. He'll say something and then there'll be this long pause, before she says something back, after which he'll fire out some muffled, probably-smooth reply. Then another long pause, and the whole thing repeats. It goes on like this for a while until I hear movement from behind the door.

I don't really like to think about what came next, if it's all the same to you. I mean sure, I'm a virgin. Let's get that out in the open right now. I never had any interest in those squalid whores on the streets below – prostitutes or otherwise – and I'm certainly not ashamed of the fact, although maybe I can only talk about it like this now since I'm dead and everything. There was only ever one woman for me, and you should know by now who that was. Once I'd made our fortune I'd planned on finding myself a wife, but not anyone from this rancid city. So yeah, I'm no fornication expert, but I know sex sounds when I hear them. What came from behind that door once Mr. Rivera and Livvy's hesitant little exchange had ended…well, *they* were sex sounds.

I, Crighton Smythe, the *leech*, turn and run back to our apartment, face burning. I slam the front door, then knock back a handful of painkillers for the earache. I grab my manuscript and sit down at the beaten up roll-top I use as my writing desk. The pain inside my ears begins to fade. In go the earplugs, out goes the world.

That's when I realized time was against me.

How many hours had I spent over the years looking in the mirror, trying to figure out when my own death was due? Too many to count, but that information was always beyond my knack. Guess that instilled in me this feeling that I had all the time in the world, but hearing Livvy and Mr. Rivera's sex sounds, the sounds of what she was doing for me, that's when I knew time was running out. I had to finish this play and start us down the path to riches. I was going to get her out of this apartment, out of this city, and away from that scumbag. It was all down to this scribbled play-in-progress in front of me. My little characters and their little lives – mother of four Kathleen Cantu and her quirky, hypochondriac, out-of-work husband Archie Cantu – were going to get us out of here.

So I got writing.

***

Livvy was pretty into all the usual God stuff, but it never really did much for me, despite what I'd tell her. Nevertheless, when you find yourself still breathing and thinking and existing after you've died, you pretty much have to believe in the afterlife. At first I thought this place might be Heaven, but then I remembered everything I'd stolen. Then I thought maybe Hell, but I'm not *that* bad a guy. So I settled on Purgatory. It's too, sort of, 'in-between' to be anything else. I mean there's others here; angels, demons, I don't know who you all are. It's not like I can see or hear anything. Sure, you've prodded and poked, maybe even tried to communicate with me, but you seem to have gotten the hint. There's only one person in the world I would ever want to talk to, and she's gone. So thankfully you mostly leave me alone, but now you give me this pen and paper? I suppose you want me to write what happened to me. I'd want to hear the story too, to be honest. I'll write it. If only because there's nothing else to do.

Crappers, I'm getting ahead of myself again. Let me tell you about when I figured out I had this knack. So I always thought I was different but never knew for sure until I saw Pa in his casket. He was attacked, you see. Pulled an extra shift on Christmas Eve and got cut up on the way home. Killed at Christmas, can you believe that? I've hated this time of year ever since. Sure, he had – as Livvy called them – 'head problems' all his life, just like her when she was a girl, but he didn't deserve this. *Racial attack*, they said. Asked a lot of questions about his head problems, as if they were to blame. Black guy with a history of mental illness?

Must have been his fault. That's how they made it out. According to Livvy, it was she that was to blame for Pa dying. She wailed like a banshee in the few days after we got the news. Then the tears stopped. I think that's when the cutting began.

They slashed his face up good, but the thing that messed with me when I saw him lying there in that damned box was the way he was patched up. *Too* patched up. He'd always had this mole on his chin you see.

Gone.

Acne scars on his cheeks?

Gone.

The folks that did him in must have sliced it all right off, leaving the mortician to rebuild a thing that *looked* like my pa, but wasn't. I remember wishing he'd been put in that casket just the way he'd been found, so that I could see him for what he really was. At least that would have been real. Guess my wish came true in a funny sort of way, seeing as ever since then my knack shows me exactly how people will die without being all patched up and fake-looking. Anyways, looking at Pa like that was when I had my first blackout. The visions and the blackouts must be linked, but I don't know how. I woke up on the floor next to the casket and there she was looking down at me, my sweet Livvy. I just lay there, gazing up into her face, listening to her soft whispers (*You all right, mon trésor? You okay?*) and suddenly out came my knack. How she'd die: it all came rushing through in that moment. I looked around at everyone else's faces as their mutterings floated over me.

And there it was. All of it.

Respiratory disease!

Pneumonia!

Suicide!

The whole damn lot, laid out in every face and voice, sledgehammer after sledgehammer in my mind.

And now that I'd tested it on poor old Baby Buggy Lady, I knew there was something to it. Thing is, I never could see how *I'd* die, no matter how long I spent looking in the mirror. Even considered for a time that could mean that I'm, well, immortal. After all, if such a thing as my knack exists, couldn't immortality? Guess I proved that theory wrong.

Anyways, so I'm sitting at my writing desk trying to get this manuscript finished. It's evening. Livvy's been back from her quality time with Mr. Rivera for a few hours. As if the thought of that wasn't bad enough, all the mad implications of my knack are bouncing around my head. (*If I can see the future, doesn't that mean everything's preordained? If I can't see my own death, am I going to live forever?*) We usually spend the evenings together, but I'm beginning to think this play might actually be the one, so I'm reluctant to stop. She's in a bit of a sulk that I'm working so late.

From my desk on the side of the room behind the couch I can see her greying, short cropped hair as she sits updating her client notebook. Like I said, she cared for old folks. Trailed herself all over looking after every old crone in this stupid city. The notebook was filled with all their names and addresses, but we'll get back to that. So she's scribbling a new client's details into her notebook when I hear her close it and drop the thing onto the coffee table. She lets out a long sigh.

'You wouldn't believe how wealthy these old dears are, Crighton.'

I hate the thought of how much money those rich, rancid old freaks are hoarding when we need it so much. I feel my face redden. I squeeze the pencil between my fingers.

'They keep it all under their mattresses for the most part, too. They tell me to pay myself, just go on in and grab what I'm due. If only they'd be more careful. Art's mother in particular. You wouldn't believe the fortune she has just sitting in that apartment.'

I squeeze harder.

'It's nice that elderly ladies like her have enough money to live their last years without financial worries. Do wish they'd enjoy it a bit more though.'

Harder.

'I suppose Mrs. Rivera's will all end up going to Art when she passes on.'

Snap.

That jackpot going straight into Mr. Rivera's slimy hands when his ma finally dies makes every muscle in my body tighten with rage. It's *us* that need money. I can't even tell Livvy about my stupid earache because we can't afford healthcare. It comes and goes, gets better then reoccurs (probably from using the same earplugs all the time) but telling Livvy would only stress her, and she's got more important things to worry about, like the soles of her shoes being worn almost to nothing, her clients, rent, and—

It's all too much. I drop the broken pencil, stand up, and walk across the living room to our tiny open kitchen. I empty the dirty dishes from the basin onto the counter. Livvy always makes me a big dinner; *the budding playwright has to keep his strength up*, apparently. As I'm filling the basin with steaming water I look at the empty peanut butter jar stuffed with utensils. Kitchen knife's been missing a while and it still hasn't turned up. I glance over at Livvy on the couch just as she's tugging the sleeves of her cardigan over her wrists, making sure the scars on her forearms she thinks I know nothing of are concealed. She spends half her life trying to cover them up. I look back at the jar and my insides contract as an image flashes through my head of what she might be using the knife for.

Livvy knows what me filling the basin means (not the dishes getting cleaned, that's for sure) so she gets herself comfy on the couch and kicks off her slippers. She lifts her feet for me as I place the basin on the floor in front of her, then groans with pleasure as I guide them into the water. She gets pretty bad aches from all the walking between clients, so I like to do this for her.

The news starts blurting out some trash about a murder. Not what you want to hear when you're trying to relax with your ma. I switch channels and all of a sudden some Christmas commercial with a Santa Claus and carol singers and kids running around is lighting up our living room. Livvy and I go silent. The air seems to freeze around us. My family (me and my ma, that is) don't talk about Christmas on account of Pa's death at this time of year. We pretend it doesn't exist, even when it's shoved in our faces. So I change channels as quick as I can and – of course, it's 8 p.m. – *Sunny Dapper Charlie's Variety Extravaganza* appears on the screen. Thank God. She's happiest when she's having her feet massaged in front of Billy Bob the Dancing Chimp or Crazy Cotton the Clumsy Contortionist or The Gummy-Wobbles Trapeze Troop. If she's happy, I'm happy. Luckily they're all on the show tonight, and thankfully it's a rerun. No Christmas stuff.

A hundred faces watch on from the apartment walls as I massage her calloused, mangled feet, except in these faces I get a break from the visions of death. Sorry, I'm talking about the photographs covering every inch of the place. Livvy was a stage actress before she had me, and most of the pictures are of her in full costume, singing or dancing or giving some impassioned monologue to a captivated audience. Still wears enough make-up to be on stage, too. Really doesn't need it though. So pretty.

Anyways, she must have been pretty good because she did quite well, but the industry soon 'spat her out', as she puts it. The highlight of her stage career was starring in a production of *Le Testament*, a short story by some French guy called Maupassant. Honestly, you've never seen someone as proud as when Livvy talks about her performance in *Le Testament*. Standing ovations, flowers thrown at her, rave reviews, you name it. That's what you get when she tells you about her run in *Le Testament*. Most importantly, she met a young black stagehand at the Grand Onyx Amphitheater. Charming guy called Laurence who ended up taking a small role in one of her plays just to impress her. She says he couldn't act to save himself, but that's what drew her to him. Too honest a man to act, she'd say. Plus she has a history of loopiness, too – psychotic episodes when she was younger and still living in Bordeaux, she's told me – so they clicked over their kookiness. Weird. Anyways, his plan worked. They got together and eventually had me. Our walls are covered with pictures of either her on stage, her and Pa, or the three of us together once I was born. There's even a couple with Clarice, our old cat. There's nothing from after my pa died, though. That's when the photographs stopped.

Okay, so back to Livvy's feet. They seem to be getting worse. The callouses feel tacked on, as if they might come off in my fingers at any moment. The blisters are like half-eyeballs staring up at me. She's ruined these feet for me, but she knows it'll be worth it. She can't see what I see, doesn't have the knack that I have, but she's told me how much she believes in my writing. She knows I'll make it big just as much as I do, and she knows it'll be worth her while. Just a bit longer in this loathsome apartment building and we'll be out. No more Pleasance Heights, no more mutilated feet, no more Mr. Art Rivera.

'We won't be here forever, Mom,' I tell Livvy, adding some gravel to the tone of my voice. Given my present situation, I don't mind telling you that, although I was twenty-five when I died, I really was just a squeaky-voiced, fat little boy. I enjoyed my time with Livvy more than anything, but the way I presented myself was still an act. Lower the pitch of my voice to sound grown up, suck in my gut, avoid the words in my head like 'jeez' and 'crappers' and 'crummy'. Odd thing for a son to do around his ma, I know. Just didn't want her to see me as the whining, pudgy kid that I was.

'Oui, Crighton,' she replies, tugging her sleeves. I lather the soapy water up her calf. 'You just keep writing your plays and you'll hit the big time soon. We're fine for now, *mon amour*. Art's good to us.'

My hands stop.

'What's wrong, son?'

Mickey Flump the Clown (*Complications from surgery, nineteen months!*) trips over his own feet, sending a cheer of applause through the audience, and crackling through our cheap set's speaker.

'Can we go up on the roof tonight, Mom?'

She pauses. 'It's been a long day, and I have clients to catch up on tomorrow since I came home early. Can it wait, love?'

'Cool,' I say, hiding my disappointment. 'Whatever. Get an early night.'

So I dry off Livvy's feet, empty the basin, and we get ready for bed. I'm sitting on the edge of the mattress brushing her hair (yes, her inch-long, greying short crop; we have our rituals, get over it) when she reaches onto her nightstand for her Maupassant short story collection, the *Le Testament* pages tattered and practically worn to nothing. You'll remember that's the short story the stage show she's so proud of was adapted from. Barely a night goes by when I don't have to read the thing to her. Don't know what I'm reading of course, on the grounds of it all being in French. But she likes it, so I like it.

'Yours is coming soon, Crighton,' she yawns once *Le Testament* is put away.

I look down at her. 'What is?'

'Your *Le Testament*.' She looks around the bedroom. Like the rest of the apartment, its walls are covered with photographs and memorabilia from the long-forgotten stage production. 'I had mine and you'll have yours. *Your* defining moment – your *Le Testament*. So long as you stay in the apartment and keep writing, it'll come.'

'I think the one I'm working on just now might be it, Mom. I have a good feeling about it.'

'Even if it isn't, your *Le Testament* will come, my love. If you don't leave, that is.'

Suppose you might think our relationship was freaky or creepy or strange. When I tell you I kissed her on the lips then got into bed with her, that we fell asleep in each other's arms, you might think we were kooky, right? Well, I don't care. Livvy was my world, and I was hers. Our love was beyond you or anyone else's approval, and I'm glad I'm dead because life was pretty lousy without her near the end, as you'll find out.

So there we are in bed, her delicate little body bundled up in my arms. Painted pine cones hang from the ceiling by threads, and even more cover every surface of the room. These are the moments I lived for, when I could nuzzle into her nightdress and let my mind wander far and wide.

My thoughts would sometimes fall on the most random things.

'Livvy, you don't need to blame yourself for what happened to Pa, and you definitely don't need to hurt yourself because of it.'

That's what I should have said. What I actually said was, 'Mom, where's the kitchen knife?'

'I'm not sure, mon chéri,' she whispers, squeezing her slender arms around me. 'It'll turn up. Sweet dreams.'

So I don't sleep so great that night and

***

Crappers, sorry. Still getting the blackouts. Who'd have thought a dead guy would get blackouts? Anyways, I guess that was as good a place to take a break as any. I'll skip forward a bit now.

A couple of weeks went by and that dumb Mr. Rivera kept appearing at the door every few nights to take Livvy down the hall to that empty apartment, but I did my best to focus on my work and not think about it. I knew my manuscript would get us out of there – it was going to be my *Le Testament*, as Livvy put it – so I worked real hard and eventually finished it. That creep was getting good at shooting me looks and steering snide comments towards me without my ma noticing. Never told her. She had enough to worry about. Overheard him trying to convince her to make me get a job and everything. 'He has a job,' she'd reply. 'He's a playwright.'

What else to tell you? Oh yeah, her clients had been overworking her, calling on her in the middle of the night and everything. It was obviously getting to her. Maybe that's why she'd started cutting again. Anyways, those old crones were just as bad as the usual vermin on the streets. Speaking of which, the news kept banging on about some spate of murders across the city. Livvy was losing her mind, drilling into me every day before she left that I was forbidden to leave the apartment, especially with all these killings. I'd go the same way as Pa if I left, apparently.

Well, hate to say it, but I did keep sneaking out around that time while Livvy was at work. Hell, we hadn't been up on the roof in so long that I had to get out of that place. Part of Livvy and Mr. Rivera's 'arrangement' was that she would care for his ma most evenings you see, meaning I got even less time with her. Besides, if you had a knack like mine you'd have wanted to test it out, too. Sure, it's pretty crummy having death shoved in your face like that, but I kept wondering whether Baby Buggy Lady was a fluke. Turns out she wasn't. My knack was real.

Anyways, I'm thinking of how I can increase the chances of my story about Kathleen and Archie's odd little family being picked up by one of the local theater companies. Our system is that once I've finished a play, Livvy will take it out with her on the way to work and drop it off with an old colleague from her theater days. I start wondering whether if I was to follow her and speak to this man myself face-to-face, make a good impression, maybe get to talk about the story with him, it might give the script more of a chance. As long as he promised not to tell Livvy I'd come, of course. I don't want to upset her again, especially since she's been under the weather recently. She's paler than usual and her voice is a bit slurry and stuff.

So there I go, slipping out of the apartment and down the landing once Livvy's left, my belly rumbling as usual at the whiff of breakfast burritos from Mr. Rivera's apartment. I sneak out onto the street, pop some painkillers, and, keeping my distance, follow her through the crowds. The plugs dampen the earache a little. I guess maybe it's the pressure that's comforting, but their most important job is to turn the sounds of the city into this kind of underwatery swishy sound, dulling the death I get from every passing voice. As for the faces, I trace the rooftops with my eyes as I walk, glancing down here and there to make sure I'm still on Livvy's tail, as they say in the cop shows. When she stops, I stop. Maybe turn stage left to have a look in a store window, taking a bite of butter as I stare into my reflection. Will this be the time I finally get to see how I'll kick the bucket?

Nope.

Anyways, poor Livvy's started limping the last couple of weeks so she's easy to keep up with. Looks like it's getting worse, too. Will need to give her feet a good seeing to this evening. Jeez, how I'd love to pick her up and just carry her away to Bordeaux.

Finally she pulls my manuscript from her tote bag. I spent all last night packaging it perfectly in brown wrapping paper, tying the string so the bow was exactly even on both sides. Got the paper real tight and it looks darned professional. I feel positive about this one. Livvy does too. She said it's 'magic' and has a really great chance, but that if it isn't accepted I can just write another which will be even better.

Figure out what's special about you, and use it, she'd said the night before. *You'll write your* Le Testament *soon enough*.

But this was the one. I could feel it.

That's when she slipped it into a garbage can.

I stood frozen, my eyes alternating between her limping away through the crowds and the garbage can. The muffled swishing of the city through my earplugs filled my head. I stood in the middle of the sidewalk, watching the most important person in my life leave what was to be my most important work in the trash, the only copy of the play that was to get us out of this place.

Pink Polka Dot Raincoat Man shoves past.

Aneurysm!

Chef on His Lunch Break swerves around me.

Car crash!

Lady in a Pantsuit knocks my shoulder.

Scuba diving accident!

I don't know how long I stood there with death upon death swimming around me, but it was long enough to watch Garbageman (*Heart failure, twenty-seven years!*) come along and empty the trashcan. I flinch as the earache rears its ugly little head, just as Garbageman dumps the trash bag in his truck and drives off with my manuscript, our supposed ticket out of here. Mother of four Kathleen Cantu and her quirky, hypochondriac, out-of-work husband Archie Cantu were gone. What was to be my *Le Testament* was gone.

And the deaths kept on swimming.

***

When she came home that night I was waiting. I'd

snapped out of my stupor and needed answers. Why had the result of all my efforts, the play she'd worked so tirelessly to allow me to pursue, been chucked away like a spent candy wrapper? Were her episodes from when she was a kid coming back? I didn't think so. I knew my Livvy, and I suspected something else was going on. I was going to find out what.

The front door opens and I leap to my feet, but before I can open my mouth Livvy stumbles into the kitchen counter. It's pouring outside, so her face is a blotchy mess of rain-ruined make-up. Standing on one foot she pulls open the drawer. The thing squeaks so loud it's like an air-raid siren. This is where she keeps her special red pen, the one she uses to cross off clients in her notebook when they die. Always know it's going to be a bad night when I hear the squeak of that drawer.

I help her limp over to the couch and take her shoes and socks off for her. I'd been working every night on that crummy manuscript, so hadn't washed her feet in a while. To be honest, she'd seemed pretty reluctant to have them washed at all lately, but she's too weak tonight to protest.

I wasn't ready for what I saw.

Jeez, it was like the fleshy tissue of her foot had ruptured through her skin. Except…it was green. Goddamn *green*. I'm not even making this up. All the veins were standing out like little blue strings, the ones running closest to the green especially bulgy. There were these blisters that I thought looked like miniature volcanoes, with gentle gradients leading up to a tiny mouth, except instead of lava, pus. This was all on Livvy. *My* Livvy.

Her sock was soaked. With what? I don't know. Blood? Pus from the miniature volcanoes? Some kind of body-juice from the green fleshy patches? I'd never seen anything like it. Her other foot wasn't so bad, but it wasn't in fine shape either.

'Mom,' I say, 'we need to get you to a doctor. This isn't good.'

She ignores me, slowly pulling her client notebook from her bag and flicking through its pages. Off comes the lid of that red pen and there she goes, scoring the neatest line you've ever seen through Mrs. Miller's name and address.

'Mom, did you hear what I said?'

'Mrs. Miller died today, and you're worried about a foot?' She stares at me. Her eyes have sunk into her head a little. Her skin is clammy and white. '*Nom de Dieu.*'

'Livvy...Mom...It looks really serious. I'm worried about—'

'You think we have the money for that kind of thing? Doctors and...and...' I notice her breathing. She's gasping as if her lungs aren't taking in any air. Her words are slurring and she's rubbing her abdomen. It must be so obvious to you that I should have done more. Why didn't I do *more*? 'Crighton, I just don't...' She tugs her sleeves as her words trail off. She's clearly exhausted. If there was ever a time to hold off questioning her about the manuscript, this was it.

Her eyes start to close.

There's a knock at the door.

She straightens.

'Settle, Mom,' I tell her. 'Rest.'

I can hear a hummed recital of *Jingle Bells* through the door. I open up, keeping the damn chain on. Peer through a slit in the door at a penguin in a Santa hat. I look up from the knitted atrocity at Mr. Rivera's weasel face.

'She's not available,' I tell him. My knowledge of his

future brain hemorrhage comforts me, but I still tense with rage at the sight of him. The rat tries to look into the apartment. I'm serious, he looks just like a beady-eyed rat. I make the tiny gap in the door even tinier.

'I haven't seen Olivia for a while. I'd hate to think you hadn't told me if anything was the matter.'

'Nothing's the matter,' I say. 'She's just not feeling well.'

'If there's anything I can do, you know I love to…' He strokes his goatee and levels his gaze. '…help.'

Brain hemorrhage! Brain hemorrhage! Brain hemorrhage!

He mouths the usual word: *leech*.

I ease the door shut. The penguin grins.

'Was that Laurence?' asks Livvy.

I stop, letting her words sink in. Laurence's my dead pa, remember. Once I've processed what she said, and recalled her telling me how confused her clients with flu can get, I turn round and answer, 'Pa's dead, Mom.' She's got the flu and that's why she's talking like this. No weird episodes, nothing serious, nothing. Nothing. At least that's what I tell myself.

Idiot.

I help her up from the couch, putting her frail arm around my neck so she can hobble to the bedroom on her good(ish) foot. I take her nightgown from the wardrobe, wondering if I'm going to have to undress her myself, but she grabs it off me and shoos me away.

'*Merci beaucoup,*' she says, sitting on the edge of the bed, 'but I can dress myself, Laurence.' She smiles a smile I've never seen. I turn slowly for the door, confused. It must be exhaustion. She's confused from the exhaustion.

She calls me back, still short on breath.

'Where's my goodnight kiss, mon chéri?'

24

I step back across the bedroom and stoop down for her usual peck on the lips, but this is no peck. Livvy…my ma…she kisses me. I mean, it lasts for maybe a second too long. There's…something. Too much *something* in her lips. I pull away, staring at her through the shadows of the dimly lit room, and tell her I'm going to write a while before I come to bed. She stands up and turns to face the wall, unbuttoning her blouse and getting ready to change into her nightgown. In a way, that was the strangest thing of all. My ma was very particular about keeping herself covered up in front of people all the time. I reach for the door as fast as I can when her soft voice suddenly pulls my attention back to the shadows.

'The knife's in my bag,' she says in a wavering, confused tone. 'Sorry you've not…you've not had it to cut the mutton with. Mutton needs cut, that's all I know. In my bag, Laurence. Knife's in my bag.' I turn away quickly as she begins to slip out of her clothes. 'All yours, mon amour.'

I close the door and go to her tote bag on the work surface. Sure enough, the kitchen knife's in there. Dried blood coats its edge.

***

The next morning, after I've spent the night on the couch, I find Livvy shivering in bed with a fever. The blinds are closed and the curtains are drawn, rendering the room as dark as the air is stale. She's completely out of breath. The sheets are soaked with sweat. She tells me it's a flu picked up from one of her clients.

'Laurence,' she says, still calling me by Pa's name, 'spend the day in the other room, will you? Can't have my handsome stagehand getting ill.'

I'm still putting her state of confusion down to the fever and do as she says. I leave some water on the nightstand next to her overflowing make-up bag and offer to change the sheets, but she waves me away. She's put socks on, so her mangled foot can't have gotten any worse. How was I to know what was happening? I'm not a doctor.

'If you need anything I'll be writing in the living room, Mom.' I'm closing the door.

'Oui,' she says, her eyes getting heavy. 'Leave your papers by the door and I'll take them out with the trash tomorrow.'

I stop.

Stepping back into the room I move through the darkness towards her, ducking around the hanging pine cones. I kneel by the bedside and run my hand over her inch-long hair. 'Mom,' I begin, knowing she's not in her right mind but that she might spill the truth as a result, 'why did you throw away my manuscript?'

'Oh, mon chéri,' she croaks, 'I do love your plays. If I had my way they'd...they'd *all* be picked up. Every stage in the country would be running them every single night. But that just can't be.'

I study her face. 'Why not? Are you trying to save me the disappointment of not making it since, well, you didn't? Is that it, Mom?'

'No, son. I'm trying to save you from being—' Her voice trails off as she searches for the words. She finds them. Her eyes widen. '—being *taken* from me.' Her shivering body tenses. Her lips tremble. Suddenly her quivering voice becomes an explosion. 'IT'S NOT *SAFE* OUT THERE, CRIGHTON.' Tears and snot and saliva begin their journeys down her face. 'You *KNOW* what happened to my Laurence, what happened all because of *me*. He was out there working so *I* could spend my time getting back on stage, so *I* could do what *I* loved, and look what HAPPENED TO *HIM*.' She's tugging her sleeves so hard they might tear. 'If you go out there, you'll go the same way as him. If your plays do well, you'll be…you'll be…' Her eyes dart around the room in confusion, then lock onto my own. '*TAKEN FROM ME*.' I try to place my hand on hers, but she yanks it away then wriggles backwards on the bed, cowering against the headboard.

I don't know what to do. I find myself wishing my ma was here to tell me how to deal with this situation, then I realize this *is* my ma. I back away slowly, the hanging pine cones moving with me on their threads before being released to swing in the darkness. I reach the door. Her sobbing bubbles away desperately from the bed.

'Can't…can't have you…*taken* from me. No, not now. Not EVER. You…you *stay* in the apartment, *YOU HEAR*? Can't…can't have you…'

I close the door and sit at my writing desk, staring at the wall. That's when I should have called an ambulance, I see that now. You don't know how much I regret doing nothing. You can't. No one can. I realize now I was a coward, the same way someone who finds a lump on their breast or balls might be too scared to see a doctor. Besides, my knack had *shown* me how my sweet Livvy was going to pass. How was I to know she was going to be the goddamn exception to the rule?! So I did nothing. Out of my own usual cowardice, I did nothing.

It's just the flu, I told myself over and over. *She'll be better soon.*

So I wrote. At least I tried to. I think I started planning a new play that day, something about a family finding their way through the usual hard times. Maybe scribbled down what I could remember of the one thrown in the garbage, too. I remember giving up eventually and sitting on the couch, staring at my reflection in the television screen.

I did check up on Livvy throughout the day, finding her asleep every time I went through. I even examined her nightdress for movement to make sure she was still breathing. If you're breathing, you're okay. That's what I thought. She didn't go to the toilet once the whole day. Guess that should have triggered alarm bells. It got to evening and I made dinner. Raided the refrigerator and ended up having a whole stew to myself with frozen fries and potatoes on the side, soaked in gravy. Didn't exactly forget about Livvy's state, but after all the stress of the day it was good to binge.

So I pass out on the couch and wake up some time after midnight. When I go through to the bedroom, which now smells pretty gross, I find Livvy in a deep sleep. Temperature's still up and she's white as a sheet. I can see she hasn't buttoned her nightgown all the way; pretty unusual for her since she's usually obsessed with being covered up and having everything fastened. I button it up for her and stand watching the fabric of her gown bounce up and down with her thumping heart. That's when I decide she's seeing a doctor the following day, whether she likes it or not. Anyways, I get into bed next to her, which she won't like on account of not wanting me to catch her flu, but I want to make sure I'll wake up if she needs anything.

What happened next is hard to write about. My ma, Olivia Smythe, was the most dignified, virtuous woman you ever could have met. I don't want to taint her memory, but you've given me this pen and paper for a reason. Everything must go down.

So I wake up in the middle of the night and…jeez, Livvy's on top of me, all right? Except…it's not Livvy. Well, it is, but not *my* Livvy. It's dark, but I can see this look on her face I've never seen before. Those eyes, they're fixed on me, but not seeing *me*. It's like she's, what do you call it? *Possessed*, or something.

Anyways, she's…straddling me, if that's how you describe it. Gyrating. I've told you how skinny she is, but her weight is somehow like a grand piano on my crotch. She must have been doing it for a while because my groin is getting sore. Don't start asking yourself *Was he? Wasn't he?* He WASN'T. Not in a zillion years did anything, you know, *happen* down there. What I mean is that I wasn't 'stimulated', if that's the word. But the worst part by far was that the buttons of her nightgown had come undone again and, well, her darned boob was hanging out. The lady that spends every waking moment fussing around making sure every bit of her is covered up, and her *boob* is out. I hate myself for thinking it, but it looked like a tatty old balloon, deflated, flapping around as she hauled herself back and forth. *Goddamn it.*

'Laurence,' she's moaning. 'Love me, *bébé.*'

I can feel her shivering as she's rocking to and fro.

'Take me, Laurence.'

She reaches down and places her blotchy hands in my own.

'You know I *want it.*'

They're cold, clammy. So cold.

'*TAKE ME.*'

I yank my hands away and push her off, leaping from the bed. She throws up on the duvet. At this point I don't know if it's all just some nightmare I'm going to wake up from. All I can do is stand there in the shadows, jaw hanging dumbly, watching her heave her guts onto the mattress. More buttons have come undone or ripped off and the back of her nightgown is slipping, exposing flesh that shouldn't be exposed. I peer through the darkness at the sliver of moonlight illuminating her sleeves and see the fabric is blotched with fresh blood. She, too, notices this and fixes her eyes on them – terror-filled eyes, eyes stretched wider than should be possible. She reaches for one of her sleeves in a motion I've seen countless times, except instead of pulling it down she begins to slowly slide the fabric back, lips trembling, face devoid of any and all color.

Upon her wrists: a criss-cross of scars and cuts, old and new, drawn right up her bony forearms in crazy overlapping intersections, a goddamn spaghetti junction of right angles etched into her flesh. I have the sudden, bizarre recollection of those meticulous red lines in her client notebook. In my mind's eye, their perfect regularity seems almost beautiful compared to the erratic madness of these carvings.

I step towards her.

She holds her defaced wrists out to me like an offering, her hands trembling violently, eyes begging for something, anything, an end to her confusion maybe, or—

She resumes her retching.

I move closer as she heaves out her insides, intending to comfort her through her hell but instead just watching as she lets everything out onto the bed. I'm hypnotized by the criss-crossing scars drawn over each scrawny wrist like two psycho games of tick-tack-toe. Her forearms, they're just...covered. She's gagging and spluttering and spitting out whatever's left as the opened cuts and gouges bleed down her wrists over her hands, flowing stigmata that won't stop, not stopping, still flowing, the blood from the criss-crosses weeping off her fingertips onto the vomit-soaked mattress. God, if there is a God, make it stop. Bring my sweet Livvy back. End this nightmare, her nightmare, our nightmare.

Criss-cross.

Criss-cross.

Criss-cross.

Make it stop *make it stop MAKE IT*—

She looks over her jagged shoulder at me. For a moment her face is nothing more than that of a blank waxwork, deadened and lifeless, until gradually the delirium returns to her eyes.

'Crighton?' she wheezes. 'What's wrong, Crighton? Why are you looking at me like that, mon trésor?'

The smell of vomit is lodged in my nostrils. My groin is still sore. Whoever that figure writhing in the darkness is supposed to be, I don't recognize her. I stumble backwards out of the room, then turn and bolt for the front door, bashing my shin off the coffee table and knocking over an open pot of pine cone paint. White and silver splash the carpet.

'Don't you go out there, son,' she calls after me. 'I'm telling you it's not *safe* out there, Crighton.'

I grab my parka, tear open the door, and lurch out onto the landing.

'Crighton? Can you hear me, Crighton? It's not SAFE.'

I slam the front door and run.

'*CRIGHTON?*'

***

I spend that night walking the streets. It's a little scary being out so late, but just as scary thinking about going home. It's cold. Luckily my gloves and hat were stuffed in my parka pockets. All my clothes are a bit small for me (my stupid chinos stop nearly halfway up my shins) but my gloves and hat and parka have always fitted me perfectly. In the breast pocket, in amongst a bed of crumbs and candy wrappers, I find an old pair of earplugs.

I keep moving, sometimes just orbiting the same block over and over. Other times I walk in a straight line for as long as I can, which is easy to do since everything around here's built in grids. My eyes keep wandering to the rooftops out of habit, but I force them back down. This city's a criminal hive at the best of times, let alone in the middle of the night, so I have to keep my eyes open. For the billionth time I reach into my pocket for a bite of butter, my hand incapable of remembering there's none. And all the while my mind keeps returning to what I woke up to, what Livvy was doing on top of me. I know she has a history of head problems, but she's been better for years. How could she just...out of nowhere...my own *ma*?

But I can't keep walking the streets forever. When the sun finally starts to come up I force my feet to take me home. Nothing else for it.

I find her sprawled out on the bed the way you might find someone sleeping in late on a Sunday morning, except she's lying face down in a mush of her own vomit. She isn't moving, her gown isn't twitching. She's like a piece of furniture: static, incapable of anything. My sweet Livvy, she's...the word is 'dead', I guess. That's all there is to say about that. She's right there where I'd left her. Dead.

Where I'd left her.

Where *I'd* left her.

Anyways, it all gets a bit blurry here. Maybe I had one of my blackouts. I remember realizing I still had my earplugs in and pulling them out, except it felt like there was still something in one of my ears. So I close the bedroom door (*maybe she just needs to lie for a little longer*), sit myself down on the couch, and start fiddling with my ear while I stare at my reflection in the television screen. Figure I need something to prod about in there, so I start rummaging about in the kitchen. Happen upon an old chopstick. That'll do. I'm about to sit back down when I realize it's 8 p.m. and time for *Sunny Dapper Charlie's Variety Extravaganza*.

I switch on the television then go back into the bedroom. Yes, the smell was unbearable, and yes, she was in just about the most inhumane state you could imagine, but (if you hadn't noticed by now) I'd gone a bit kooky. All I knew in that moment was that if I buttoned up her nightgown and got her in front of *Dapper Charlie's*, everything would be all right.

So I carry her through and plonk her down on the couch. I'm tipping the dirty dishes out of the basin as usual, filling it with steaming water while the theme tune to our favorite show is blaring through the television's crackly speakers. Before I know it there I am, massaging the ruined feet of a corpse in front of *Sunny Dapper Charlie's Variety Extravaganza*, laughing my head off at Billy Bob the Chimp trying to juggle just one too many oranges at the same time. Seems like he's more interested in eating them! There they go, rolling off the stage and into the audience. Oh, but he does look great in his sailor's outfit, especially when he takes a low bow to the applause. I'm just about wetting myself with laughter at this. It really is quality television.

Then I realize Livvy isn't laughing.

Figure I should stop rubbing her feet and look up to ask her what's wrong (she usually splits her sides laughing over Billy Bob the Chimp) but somehow I just can't bring myself to do it. Before long I'm finding it hard to laugh at all, until finally I pluck up the courage to look at her.

Her droopy-eyed face suddenly tips forward, just the way it used to when she'd fall asleep in front of the television. Her jaw was never twisted into this lifeless contortion though, and I'd never seen her skin this porcelain white. For some reason I feel compelled to look down at her breast, the same one to have fallen out when I woke up to her...well, you know...but I stop myself. I force my gaze to the army of painted pine cones on the sideboard instead until, beyond my control, my eyes sink slowly to the basin of water on the floor. I've not yet looked at the abomination I've been massaging, so lost have I been in my fantasy. I take hold of the ankle and raise her bad foot from the basin.

The first of many burst blisters is just about to break the water's surface when there's a knock at the door.

'Olivia and I have an arrangement, Crighton,' Mr. Rivera says once I get up and open the door to a slit. It's a miniature woolen fireplace with stockings hanging from its mantelpiece today. I wipe my hands on my trousers. 'You're too young to understand, but I'm doing a lot for your family. Far more than *you*, anyway. I'm going to have to insist on seeing her.'

He pushes on the door but I press my pretty substantial weight against it, keeping it in place. Forgot to put the chain on. I do it now. 'I told you before,' I tell him, staring right into that sleazy face, 'my ma's not feeling well.'

Our eyes remain locked for a few long seconds, then he

breaks the staring match and turns to walk down the landing. Looking over his shoulder he says, 'This is *my* building, and you're *my* tenants.' Then, with a smile, 'Rent's due end of the month.'

Okay, so as you've gathered, I went a bit nutty around this time. I won't apologize for it. Not you, Mr. Rivera, nor anyone has ever had anything like what Livvy and I had, so it's not your fault you won't understand what came next. All I remember after closing the door on that bonehead is deciding that I wouldn't let anyone get to my ma. I'd protect her from him, from all those old crones, from this vermin-filled town – from everyone. I stopped caring what she'd done with my manuscript. I get she was just protecting me from an industry that had chewed and spat her out, and from the city. She worked so hard just to keep me writing behind a closed door where she knew I'd be safe. Hell, if I could have done the same for her you'd better believe I would have. Might have kept her from dying. My sweet Livvy protected me the only way she knew how, and now I could think only of protecting her.

So I put on my roof gear – parka, hat, gloves, the whole shebang. Then I gear Livvy up for the cold, slipping her hands through the sleeves of her big beige raincoat and popping on her own hat and gloves. We were well overdue some roof time together.

It's a struggle, that's for sure, but like I keep telling you I'm a strong guy. Everyone always thought I was just fat, but there's muscle in there, let me tell you. Besides, she's real thin. I carry her up the ladder and out our roof access where we always have two deckchairs set up. We used to love sitting out there, gazing up at the stars. She used to tell me my pa was looking down on us. I never believed in God and all that stuff, despite what I'd tell Livvy, but I have to say I did like the thought of Pa watching over us.

So we lie next to each other on the deckchairs, just like we used to. Livvy has her favorite blanket over her and I have a fresh block of butter. I stare into the night sky above us, my eyes skipping tirelessly between the starry white pinpricks in the endless black.

I think of the rent Mr. Rivera says is due at the end of the month, pressing the heels of my hands into my aching ears. I can't get a normal job on the grounds of my blackouts, and Livvy's not quite well enough to support me at the moment. I still believe in my scripts, it's just that apparently theater execs don't look in trashcans for potential winners. I need to get writing so I can make my fortune and get us out of here, just as I always planned to, but I *need* to make sure it's good enough. Despite where I now know all my work ended up, I always had a feeling my stuff was lacking something. It was too *samey*. I need to write something...different. Something that will make people sit up and take notice. The clock's ticking.

I look over at Livvy. She's so beautiful in the moonlight, completely at peace.

Figure out what's special about you and use it, she'd said. *You'll write your* Le Testament *soon enough.*

Something clicks.

...what's special about you.

Then it hit me. My knack was what made me special. Yes, it's a curse, but how many other people could do what I do, see in a face or hear in a voice exactly how someone was going to die? You're not given a power – yes, a *power* – like that for no reason. I can write a new play, a darker play, and have it center around my knack. The kind of vermin this city's full of will lap that stuff up, a play all about death. Yeah, I'll just write about a guy with the same knack as me and how he copes with his visions of death. They'll eat that up and then I'll be able to get Livvy out of here. I just need a little time to write it.

Rent's due end of the month.

I tuck the blanket around Livvy then head back down the roof access. I chuck some painkillers down my throat, take the red pen from the drawer, then the client notebook from her tote bag, and flick through the endless list of names and addresses.

Maybe some of these wrinkly hags with fortunes under their mattresses (fortunes they'd never know what to do with even if they had all the time in the world) are on their way out soon. Maybe with the addresses in this notebook I can get close enough to see when they're due to die. Maybe it wouldn't be so wicked to take some cash out of their hands. Only once they'd passed on, of course. The scumbags of this city would only blow their inheritance on drug habits or hookers, anyways. No, I can put it to good use. I can give Livvy back what she's owed after all her years of slaving away, after giving her *life* for those old crones.

I pull the lid off the red pen.

Everything's going to be all right, Livvy.

***

So the next day I leave the apartment with Livvy's client notebook. I take the earplugs out of my jacket pocket, but stop before sticking them in.

Breast cancer!
Rectal cancer!
Eye cancer!
Choking on a Slush Puppie!

The sound of the city is already filling my brain, its streets filled with promises of death only I can discern. I put the earplugs back in my pocket and stand in the middle of the sidewalk, watching the doomed masses swarm around me. Demise upon demise flows through my head, but I take it. If my next play – my *Le Testament* – is going to be about my knack, then I'm going to have to get inspiration from somewhere.

I walk.

I found a scarf parceled up the night before in the apartment. Seems like Livvy knitted it herself. I think I can smell her on it. She always gave me a gift around this time of year, never on Christmas though. It's always a few weeks before or after. Like I said, we don't talk about Christmas. Anyways, the scarf keeps the lousy endless snow from getting under the neck of my parka. I nuzzle into its thick purple wool and take a good whiff, then press on through the rabble.

I cover the notebook with my gloved hand, protecting it from the snow. These pages are much more valuable than regular notebook pages. I squint down at the list of names and addresses. The rest of the week will be spent trudging around the city tracking down these places, the homes of Livvy's clients. I'll only manage one or two a day, whereas she used to cover a half dozen in one shift. She must have walked even further than I imagined – then again, she didn't have to ask for directions as much as I do. The plan is that once I arrive I'll press the building buzzer until I get a reply and make up some excuse about forgetting my key. That's if it's an apartment building. If it's a house, I'll sneak up to their living room window, or even look through their mail slot until I see them walking through their hallway. However it plays out, I'll only need to catch a glimpse of each old crone's face to see the info I need: the time of their death. Then, when the time's right, I'll come back to collect.

As for how they'll die, it'll be mostly the same from client to client. Pneumonia, cardiac arrest, whatever. Not important. They'll all end up stiff as a plank in their bed or slumped over in their armchair in front of *Days of Our Lives* anyways. All I'll need is the date and time, which will get scribbled next to their names in the notebook, then off I'll go on my rounds. I can only hope there's some due to die sooner rather than later. Need my rent money.

But that's the week to come. Who'd have thought that this, the first day of my little mission, I'd hit the jackpot.

A Mrs. Josephine Sudworth, the very first client whose home I call at, is adjusting her television antenna when I spy her through the sheer curtains of her living room window. I can hear her grandfather clock chiming from inside. I stare at her face and can't believe my luck; by the end of the afternoon she'll be dead as a dodo on her couch. Heart attack. What are the chances?

So I went for a plate of fries in a diner I'd passed down the street, following up with a slice of apple pie, then a second dessert of chocolate ice cream. There was still a little time on old Mrs. Sudworth's clock, so after a quick pretzel and extra helping of fries I made my way back to her little bungalow. I looked through those thin curtains and saw the back of the couch, with Josephine's white hair just visible, the television casting a flickering light around the room, blaring its noise, rendering the chiming grandfather clock barely audible. She didn't appear to be moving. I wondered whether she maybe had kids or grandkids she'd planned on leaving her dough to. Then I thought of Livvy's feet and how she'd ruined them for crones like this, and for such little pay or gratitude. Barely ever got tipped, too. Lost most of her wages on social security for old bats like these, but I bet Mrs. Sudworth didn't plan on leaving anything to Livvy, that's for sure. No, I made up my mind that I was owed this money. My ma always wanted to be able to leave me something, and I figured this would have to be it. I knew what I was going to do was the right thing.

So I did it.

I took a bite of butter and ditched the wrapper in a bush, before approaching the front door and trying the handle. Locked. So I went around and tried the back door. Locked, of course. Finally I found a window half open I could just about squeeze through if I sucked in my gut. Didn't need to worry too much about noise since I knew by this time she'd be stone-cold dead. I started feeling dizzy, the way I do before a blackout, so I took a moment to calm myself and force it away. Guess anyone would feel funny breaking into someone's house like this. Anyways, before I knew it there I was, standing over Mrs. Sudworth's expired face, with that damned grandfather clock chiming again. *Chime, chime,* goddamn *chime.*

Can't say she looked particularly peaceful. One eyelid was half-closed, while the other stared up at me all wide and freaky. Her mouth was sort of gnarled into a wacky shape. Guess heart attacks can't be all that great a way to go. I switched off the television. Couldn't take the racket.

So all there was left to do was get to work. I checked all the obvious places, starting with under her mattress. Some of Livvy's clients trusted her so much they would let on where their cash was kept, telling her to help herself to her day's wage.

Chime...

Of course she'd have no reason to write that in her notebook (sure would have made my life easier) but she did mention a few times how obscure some of the hiding places would be.

Chime...

Never where you'd expect, she'd said.

Chime...

Yet always right in front of you.

Chime...

I turned to the grandfather clock.

Massive hulking thing it was, big gothic brute. I swung open its door, taking some pleasure in stopping its pendulum with my hand. The incessant ticking ceased. I fished around its dusty interior, hoping I wouldn't get bitten by some bug or whatever the hell was probably living in there. Wedged a couple of splinters into my fingers before I felt the fake bottom jiggle under my hand. I reached in and found a little wooden jut I could lift the base with, and voila! Hadn't known what to expect in terms of quantity, or even if I'd find her stash at all, if there was one. Would it have covered this month's rent Mr. Rivera was nagging me for? I had no way to know, but as soon as my hand found the stash in that grandfather clock I immediately knew rent wasn't going to be an issue.

I picked every last crumpled bill out of there and stuffed it all in the several pockets of my parka, then replaced the base, set the pendulum swinging again, and closed the hinged door. I stepped back around the front of old Mrs. Sudworth to say my final goodbyes.

Livvy would have wanted this, I told myself. I still believe she would have wanted me to take the money. I don't regret anything I did before I died, but can't say I didn't feel a little bad for poor Josephine Sudworth sitting there all stiff and twisted while some chubby fat-ass ran off with her savings.

I switched the television back on. Her show hadn't finished, luckily. Guess she could still catch the end. Least I could do.

On the way out I noticed one of Livvy's painted pine cones sitting pride of place on the window sill. That made me smile. I got out the client notebook, scored a red line through old Josephine's name, then exited stage right.

First collection: done.

***

So I trail back across town to Pleasance Heights. Mr. Rivera's on the landing down from our apartment overseeing a workman with a yellow hard hat messing around with the ceiling, so I stop to give him his stupid cash.

'My ma told me to give this to you,' I say to him.

He looks down at the money in my outstretched hand, stroking his goatee in his usual smarmy way. 'I've not seen her go to work in a while, Crighton.'

'Still under the weather.'

There's a pause while the bonehead looks me up and down. Part of me likes how little he thinks of me. Used to hear him banging on to Livvy about how I should get a job, how at my age he was working every hour God gave him, how hard his family slaved to take ownership of this building, blah blah blah. Way I saw it, if a creep like him hated me then I must have been doing something right.

'Your rent is going up,' he says, delicately picking a speck of dust from the grotesque knitted Christmas-turkey-on-a-baking-tray covering his torso.

Brain hemorrhage!

'Olivia and I had an arrangement, and she's not kept to that arrangement.'

Brain hemorrhage!

'Tell her another fifty bucks a month should do it. I have a catalogue of upkeep costs to consider, you understand.'

Brain hemorrhage! Brain hemorrhage! Brain hemorrhage!

I feel my face going red. I hate that it does that. I reckon I'm pretty good at keeping my cool, but my stupid fat face always lets the side down. It's a darned betrayal, your own face giving the game away like that.

He smiles.

'Your mother probably never told you, but the pair of you have somewhat of a…backlog. I'm afraid it's time to pay up. Let's call it a round four hundred by the end of the week.' He adjusts his glasses. 'Or, young Smythe, you're out.'

And with that Mr. Rivera casually turns back to Yellow Hard Hat Man and continues discussing his stupid ceiling, as if I was a fly he'd swatted away. I can feel the blood pulsating through my face. I march down the landing as quick as I can before my face explodes or I lunge at the guy or something.

I'm flicking through the notebook while I pace the apartment, trying to weigh up whether the kind of money he's talking about is even possible. Mrs. Wilson's due to drop dead in a fortnight, but that's too late. Mr. Rodriguez will trip over his slippers and crack his head open on the sideboard shortly after that, but again, too late. I can't believe my luck with all these handy deaths, but my collections just aren't soon enough. Can't move out either or else Livvy will be taken from me. Besides, even if I could somehow bring her with me, it's not easy to find a place with the kind of roof access I'd need to keep her, let alone the task of actually moving her all the way to a new…blah, blah, blah. That's where my head was by this point. Leave Pleasance Heights and she'll be Mr. Rivera's for good: that was my assessment of the situation. Yeah, looking back I'd gone a bit nuts, but loopiness ran in my family, so hey-ho.

Anyways, there I was pacing back and forth, my thoughts going round and round trying to figure out where this cash was going to come from, when there's an almighty scream.

From the roof.

'Holy FUCK, what the *hell* is…what the…' bellows Yellow Hard Hat Man as I clamber up through the roof access. 'Jesus mother of *FUCK*.'

He drops his hardhat and dashes through the snow (in a one-horse open sleigh), leaving his tools strewn over the white-capped roof, then scrambles down the access. I wander over to Livvy. Once Y.H.H.M. has tumbled back into the building, Mr. Rivera's head pops up. His eyes immediately find my own, then they drop to the corpse laid out on the deckchair by my side.

Guess the details must have come to him gradually as he approached me and my ma. I stood frozen, not knowing quite what to do next. By now my face was probably about ready to blow, glowing a dark crimson. Anyways, she'd have looked normal enough from back at the roof access. Strange sight I imagine though, a supposedly ill woman lying wrapped in blankets on some deckchair on the roof in the falling snow. But I guess Livvy's withering face would have become clearer the closer he got and, to be honest, it was a bit of a mess. Luckily I'd fixed her make-up the night before.

So I follow his gaze down to Livvy and end up looking right into her eyes, eyes burrowing into crusty eye-shadowed sockets like a couple of round watery bugs. Jeez, I can still see that deteriorating excuse for a face, peering out through a light covering of snowfall. I'd been spending every night on the roof with her (I was due them, after all) but I guess the reality of what had happened to her, of her lifelessness, had somehow been escaping me. Now that I could see the effect she was having on people, the reality hit home. No escaping it now.

I turn back to Mr. Rivera. I feel the blood throbbing in my face. His own has gone completely white, and not from the snow.

'You can't have her,' I scream, shaking, feeling about ready to explode from my own body. 'STAY AWAY!'

The snow dances around the odd congregation. I stand firmly between Rivera and my beloved, sweet, dead ma. At that moment I thought of leaping to my death with her, soaring from the rooftop to the streets below, just so we could be obliterated together. Anything but have her fall into his hands.

But I didn't. I'm a coward, so I didn't. I just stood there, wailing and crying and shaking with rage.

'Stay away! Keep your hands *off* her!' Carol singing echoed up from the streets below, the soundtrack to my screams. 'You can't have her – *STAY AWAY!*'

***

And that was that. Last thing I remember was screaming my head off on the rooftop feeling like my face was going to explode, then nothing. Must have blacked out. They took Livvy from me, the cops and paramedic people and whoever else. Cause of death: sepsis. Blood poisoning from the wound on her foot, I'm told. They asked if she'd behaved in any way strange when she took ill, since sepsis-associated ence— ...encefal— ...encephalopa— ...well, whatever the word was, can cause episodes in people with a history of psychosis, like my ma. Told them nope. No weird behavior. They could never understand what she went through, the pain and confusion she endured. All because those damn old crones just had to have her every minute of every day, making her walk far and wide until her foot split open and killed her. Whoever died from *walking*? From *helping people*?!

Mr. Rivera announced that he'd *Let Crighton stay at Pleasance Heights for free for as long as he needed to get himself sorted.* Sounds darned nice on the face of it I'm sure, but you didn't see his face as he said it. The only reason he wanted the *leech* to hang around was so he could taunt him and pester him into getting a job and undermine him at every turn and make him feel generally crummy about himself. No, there was nothing nice about his offer. I thanked the creep, thanked the police, thanked the ambulance crew, thanked everyone that dragged my sweet Livvy away from me, then left. Just...left. Never realized how easy it would be. Without Livvy at home in our apartment, I could just walk out. You know I never even went to her funeral, which I believe *he* was going to arrange. No way was I going to give him the satisfaction of going along to a service *taken care of* by the wonderful Mr. Art Rivera. I'd pay tribute to Livvy in my own way.

Nope, just shoved some stuff in a bag and left. Exit downstage right.

Where did I go? Well, didn't have much cash on the grounds of giving that weasel everything I'd collected from

Mrs. Sudworth, so I slept rough. With the vermin of the city, I slept rough. Every spot that looked halfway acceptable for a night's sleep was taken; bandstands in the park, bus shelters, underpasses, all filled with dirty, scum-ridden hobos. Winter had settled good and proper, with the darned snow and frost not letting up for one second. Crappers, those nights were cold. I thought of the bed I shared with Livvy, her body wrapped around me, its warmth an infinite blessing. I'd have killed to be there at that moment. As it was, all I had of her was a painted pine cone in my pocket. I still nuzzled into that scarf, trying to salvage even the faintest whiff of her to take my mind off the cold and the hunger and the worsening earache. But I was fooling myself. Her scent was gone. Even the paint on the pine cone was chipping away. God knows what they'd do with her body. Burn or bury it, I guess. Every trace of her was soon to vanish. Mr. Rivera would no doubt have the apartment emptied before long, all the framed photographs of our little family's history wiped off the face of the Earth. I should have cared more about all that, taken what I could. There's a lot I should have done, but I didn't. As usual, I was a coward.

Anyways, I found this spot under a bridge. Sure, it had stinking hobos there just like everywhere else, but at least these ones were either unconscious or in a drunken daze. There was this one guy tucked away in an empty recess with a thick tweed overcoat and blankets all around him. This bum had won the lottery, by hobo standards. His muddied, festering face told me he was due to bite the dust the following night. Parka wasn't really cutting it in this weather, so I came back and took his loot once I was sure he was a goner. Felt the usual dizziness, like a blackout was coming, but was all right. I really didn't have the nerve for this thieving business.

So I find a little corner of my own to hunker down in for the night. Mr. Rivera's been plaguing my thoughts all day, the snake. The only thing I think about as much as his sorry face is my sweet Livvy. Sitting there in the lousy rain and snow, gales biting my skin as I try desperately to slip into sleep, I see her as an angel, and angels aren't meant to die, are they? Angels don't get blood poisoning. Besides, I'd *known* how she was going to go. She was meant to pass away decades from now surrounded by the family I'd raise, having lived a life of luxury made possible by the success of my plays. I'd known how *everyone* was going to go – and I'd been right – so why was I wrong about her? Stupid sepsis. What the *hell*? That hadn't been part of the plan! Damn my knack.

Eventually I give up on sleep and gather my blankets, then start walking in what I thought was a random direction. Of course, I end up right back at Pleasance Heights. So there I am, standing on the street, that bum's piss-stained blanket wrapped around me, looking up at the window of our old apartment. I move my gaze across the wall of the building to the Rivera place. I see a hunched over silhouette shuffling across the window, no doubt the outline of his own ma. She never leaves their apartment. I can taste the paella probably simmering away on their stove right now. My stomach rumbles.

Right, so that's me, standing there wrapped in a crusty old sheet, an orphan, staring up at a life long gone. I haven't touched my manuscript in days, what with everything that's been going on, but if I don't finish my *Le Testament* then how am I going to get out of this rat-infested hole of a city? Everything's changed, and yet nothing has. I still have to write a script worth something;

make some dough, get out of this town. Maybe find my way to Bordeaux. Livvy always wanted to go back there. She's gone, but I still have to do all this for her. But how can I write on the streets? And what about food? I'll starve if I don't get some cash quick, and don't get me started on the aching in my ears. Feeling about ready to rip them off my head. Need more painkillers. Crappers.

I sit myself down on the sidewalk and flick through the now-tatty client notebook, skimming through the death dates. (*Death dates…* Catchy, huh?) Finally, some luck: a Mr. Wayne Mitchell has a blood clot in his brain gearing up to take the old guy out in just under a week. So over the coming days I make my way slowly across town towards his apartment building, sleeping rough at a different spot each night. By the time the day of his death rolls round I'm practically sleeping on his doorstep. I make up some baloney about being locked out and get buzzed up. I got this man's death date weeks ago by peering through his mail slot and seeing his face as he stood in his hallway on the telephone. I also checked for a spare key, and sure enough I found one on the ledge above his door. These old folks really ain't too sharp.

Anyways, by this time I'd spent all my cash on food. Mr. Mitchell's little stash (taped on the underside of a cabinet this time – ingenious) was a godsend. Drew a red line through his name then headed for the nearest diner, where I gorged on two lasagnas and a big creamy cheesecake. I'd been having to tighten my belt as the weight fell off me without Livvy's meals, so it was magnificent to finally feed like this.

I got a subway back across town and took a takeout into the little recess I'd found previously. I hunkered down with my blanket and set about tearing into one of the four hamburgers I'd picked up at a Red Barn, stuffing the fries and onion rings into the buns and squishing them into the burgers.

'What's that, kid? Supper?' The voice came from above. I look up from my little nest and see three hobos looking down at me. If it hadn't been so dark I'd probably have been able to see them salivating down their chins. At the burgers or me? You decide.

I nod and offer a burger up to them as I stealthily button up my overcoat pocket. If I have to do a runner I can't have old Mr. Mitchell's cash falling out all over the sidewalk.

They ignore the burger.

Hobo #2 says, 'Why you on the streets if you be affordin' all that?' He spits a yellow globule onto the sidewalk, then continues, 'He's struck it good, that's what I'm thinkin'.' The streetlight catches the network of scars on his cheek. The image of Livvy's scar-covered wrists flashes through my mind. *Criss-cross, criss-cross, criss-cross.* How could her cutting have gotten so bad? Why did it start up again? Why would—

'Something to do with what's in his pocket. Ain't that right, kid?' the third one says, stepping forward.

So there you go. I got mugged. By a bunch of scumbag bums, no less. Don't get me wrong, I put up a fight. I'm a big guy and I really threw my weight around, enough for them to curse and back off here and there, but I was no match. They pinned me down, got their filthy, thieving hands on Mr. Mitchell's dough, and scuttled off to fight over who got what. Hobo #1 had smacked me over the back with a pipe and Hobo #3 had kicked me square in the ribs, so I was all out of fight.

Have to say, lying in that recess with blood all over my

face, writhing in agony on the ground, I didn't give a second thought to the money they'd gotten away with. All that was in my mind was Livvy.

Before I knew it, I was limping through the night towards Pleasance Heights. What was any of it worth without my sweet Livvy? This play that was supposedly going to make me so rich – my *Le Testament* – that was all for her. To get us out of this city, to give her the life she deserved, to pay her back for all she'd done. But now she was gone, so what was the point? As I dragged myself through the streets, now no different from the vermin of the city I loathed so much, all I could see in my mind's eye was that rooftop where my Livvy should still have been lying.

Then I was there.

I can't even remember much of it. I must have forced the latch on the rear entrance, then used the roof access on the landing. I always was quiet, Livvy and Pa had said back in the day. Quiet as a fox.

All that mattered was that I was back on our rooftop. I clambered across the roofs to where our deckchairs still sat, then dropped to my knees by Livvy's and stared at the space where she should have been. I peered through the darkness at the blue and white striped fabric of the deckchair and saw the stain, the only remaining mark of my perfect Livvy, just a lonesome little patch where her poor body had lain all those days and nights. A *stain*. That's all they left of her, the vultures. I leant down and held my nose to the stain, breathing in the only part of Livvy left in this world.

'*It's the MOST – wonderful tiiiiiime – of the year!*'

The sudden singing makes me jump. I spin around, still on the ground, and look up at Art Rivera.

'Are you getting a good whiff, Crighton?' He tuts, shaking a finger at me. 'You're leeching off her even after she's dead and buried. Naughty little leech.' His eyebrows raise in that slimy, condescending way. 'Can't let sleeping dogs lie, huh?'

'Why don't you…just…why can't—'

'Never were great with words, were you Crighton? Not good for a supposed playwright.'

He steps closer. I wrap my arms around the deckchair to protect it, and with it the stain. Mr. Rivera towers over me.

'You made your choice. I offered to keep you rent-free until you finally got a job and did something with yourself. Not that I ever could see that really happening.' He scratches his goatee. I feel my face burning. 'As things stand, you're trespassing.' He crouches in front of me, those poky little eyes poised inches from my face. 'Festive salutations, my chubby little leech. Now get the fuck off my property.'

I'd spend many nights imagining what I could have said or done at that point. Should I have swung for him, smashed the deckchair over his head, or simply launched my weight in his direction? I'd lie awake both pleasuring and torturing myself over what may have been, but in the end none of it matters, because I cried. I cried endless, pathetic tears, pouring over my pudgy cheeks as I scurried to the roof access and dropped back down onto the landing. Did I hear him laugh as I tumbled away? Who knows. Again, doesn't matter. What matters is what I saw as I stumbled down that gloomy landing towards the staircase.

There I went, stomping through the darkness, the world blurred with tears. That's when the hunched old woman appeared. Nearly mowed her down, too. I wiped my eyes and gazed into that face, framed by long, curly white hair. She was nearly as pretty as Livvy, despite her age. Everything fell away in that moment: the smell of Mexican food making my stomach rumble; Dean Martin singing *Baby, It's Cold Outside* from the open door of the Rivera place; the door of another apartment at the other end of the hall, *the* apartment, where Rivera used to take Livvy; the new nameplate on me and my ma's old door. All of it just disappeared. All I saw was a stroke, clear as day in this old lady's face. A stroke on New Year's Eve.

She smiles at me, but her affection rides on an undercurrent of elderly confusion. She's a kind one, this I can tell. Just like Livvy. I smile back and for the briefest moment, all of the pain and anger and uncertainty disappears. For an instant, I have my Livvy back.

'Mama,' Rivera calls from behind her. 'Get away from him, Mama. Go back inside.'

So this is Mrs. Rivera.

I look over her stooped shoulders at the rat, who hurries towards us to usher her away from me. Little old me. Little harmless Crighton Smythe, the fat leech who'll pay another visit to Pleasance Heights on New Year's Eve. The flabby leech who'll take poor Mr. Rivera's inheritance from this lovely elderly lady – the same elderly lady Livvy had cared for, and the same inheritance she'd told me was so sizable. And this old lady won't mind. Eyes as kind as these would be sympathetic to what I've been through, and, more importantly, what her son has done to me and my ma.

Yes, little Crighton will finally have the money to get out of this diseased, scum-laden city. He'll take the memory of his dearest Livvy with him, back to Bordeaux to where she always wanted to return, where he'll have the peace and comfort to finish his *Le Testament*. It all comes back to money, and in this sweet, expiring old woman he'll find that money. And let's not forget, as an added bonus, Mr. Art Rivera will have it stuck to him one final time when his inheritance is yanked away from him.

The tears stop. I shoot Art a look sharper than any look he'd ever shot me. I mouth the words *bye-bye inheritance*, then turn and stride down the stairs and into the night.

Okay, I don't. I scamper silently away like I always do.

Never mind. I had work to do.

***

So what do I tell you now? We're nearing the end of my story, so I better make these final pages count.

It was pretty much a waiting game after my little run-in with old Mrs. Rivera. New Year's Eve, that's when she was going to die. I was going to slip in, acquire her sizable nest egg, and finally get me out of this dive of a city, as well as depriving her rat son of his inheritance.

So it's mid-December, with only a couple of weeks before all that's due to go down. I busy myself in the meantime by working through any more collections in Livvy's client notebook due before New Year, keeping my eyes peeled for any bonus death dates in the people I pass. The streets are getting busier with Christmas shoppers, not to mention 'Nam protesters. The mindless scurrying of the shoppers, and empty preaching of the equally mindless protesters, say nothing to me but death.

Liver failure!
Kidney failure!
Gunshot wound!

Drowning at the seaside!

My head's beginning to overflow with death. It's a misery, but I endure.

At this point I'm still finding it hard to believe how lucky I am in finding so many death dates right when I need them. Once I've picked up another collection or two and have the funds, I move myself into a dingy room in a grimy old hotel directly opposite Pleasance Heights, owned by this sloshed old creep – call him Drunken-Stupor Man. He mostly just leaves me alone and sits drinking at his desk in the 'lobby' (as with Pleasance Heights, that makes it sound way fancier than it is). So what do I have in that rancid little cell? A damp mattress on the floor and a rotting old corner desk, on which I arrange my newest manuscript work in progress, the client notebook with its red pen, and one of Livvy's painted pine cones. On the floor by the mattress: the Maupassant short story collection, left open at *Le Testament*.

On the wall I pencil a makeshift calendar for the coming weeks, and cross off each day leading up to New Year's Eve. By day I go out collecting. People pay less attention to you during the day. They're too caught up in their own business. By night I try to write, but there's too much going on in my mind to concentrate properly. Mostly I just sit at the grubby window, looking out across the street at the Rivera apartment, holding out for the hunched silhouette of poor old Mrs. Rivera, trying to catch a glimpse of her wrinkly old face so I can confirm what I already know. Sometimes my eyes stray across the building to our old window, which has its own new set of silhouettes shuffling around. And all the while I nuzzle into that woolen scarf, dragging from it every last scent of Livvy I imagine it still holds.

But of course, there's no more Livvy in that scarf.

There's no more Livvy.

Anyways, the cash I'm stashing under my mattress is mounting up. Getting to be quite a lumpy thing, but it doesn't matter since I'm barely sleeping. Try to keep myself awake as much as possible due to these dreams I keep having, horrible nightmares about...well, you know. What happened with my ma that night. But I don't want to talk about that again.

So as much as I hate the snow and the cold, it seems like the weather's working in my favor on the grounds of all the pneumonia going around the elderly folks. The hags are dropping like flies. Works for me. I should mention that I did consider whether I should be using my knack to help them. You know, see when they're due then leave an anonymous note, telling them to have someone with them on this day at this time. But who am I to interfere with nature? Besides, for the most part they're being knocked off by stuff no one could really do anything about. Blood clots, hemorrhages, heart attacks: they're screwed no matter what way you look at it. And, like I said, they owe Livvy and me.

When I was a kid, and before Pa died, we'd go for these family nights out to the theater. You know, pretty much see whatever was on, just to try get me into all that stuff while I was still young. Well, this one night we messed up the times. Ended up getting in just as the final scene was playing out. Can't even remember what production it was, but I do remember being taken again some weeks later. Thing was, I didn't give a darn what happened to any of the characters. See, I knew how the finale was going to play out, how it was all going to end. Mr. what-dya-call-it was going to get with Miss what's-her-name, and the evil whatever-his-face would get what was coming to him. I didn't worry about any of their trials and tribulations along the way. I'd seen the ending.

So you see, that's how I felt before Livvy died. I knew (or thought I knew) how and where she was going to pass away. She'd die in a nice big house surrounded by the family I'd raise once my plays had made me more money than I could ever spend. I knew the ending. Our trials and tribulations: who cares? Fate was real. All I had to do was let it play out.

But then *it* happened, the goddamn sepsis. All from *walking*. She was taken from me, and far earlier than my knack had told me. Was there nothing to my visions after all? No, there had to be, especially since I was now basically making a living out of expired old crones. Nevertheless, now I'd seen how easily things could be taken out of my hands. I knew this was the time for determination. I accumulated as much cash as I possibly could until my little mattress was practically touching the ceiling. I walked those streets, earplugs out, eyes on every passerby, looking out for impending death dates I could take advantage of. I reckon all this exercising of my knack was strengthening it, because the death flooding into my head was increasing in strength and range. It was like I could see the entire city's destinies of death. It had always felt like a curse, regardless of how I was managing to make use of it, but at this rate it was seeming like it might grow out of my control. Could my mind take such massive influxes of death? Crappers, I wasn't sure.

But, like I say, I tried to take advantage of my infliction in as many ways as possible. From my visions I gathered as much inspiration as I could for my next play. My *Le Testament* was going to be about a guy just like me, fighting through life knowing what I know, being told what I'm told by every face and every voice to come his way. I guess I'd had many potential *Le Testaments* up to this point, many failed ones (or rather, ones thrown in the trash) but never had I felt so sure about an upcoming work. Once I could focus on its writing, that would be it.

And at night I kept myself awake, imagining all the freedom I'd have after New Year's Eve.

***

Right, let me skip forward to the night before old Mrs. Rivera was due to croak, since something kind of odd happened.

I'm sitting at the window watching the Rivera apartment, popping painkillers for the growing goddamn earache, when something makes me freeze. What was that? Two little blinking lights coming from the side of the drapes hanging around the Rivera window. I squint through the driving snow to try and spot them again.

Binocular lenses.

Brain hemorrhage!

I drop down out of sight, my face already blazing with the sudden rush of blood. Slowly I try to peer over the windowsill, but there's nothing there. Weird, huh? Anyways, that's kind of important so don't forget.

***

New Year's Eve arrives. I'm too excited to sit still. (Yeah, excited for the death of an old lady. So sue me.) I slip past Drunken-Stupor Man's desk and spend the day pacing the streets through driving gales. The last collection I hopefully ever have to make is imminent, so I treat myself and pop in my earplugs. I walk for miles. Been doing a lot of that lately. Going to get skinny if I'm not careful.

I also treat myself to a big meal, then a fresh block of butter for old time's sake, before continuing my march all around town, chomping away, trying to think up all the places Mrs. Rivera might hide her stash. Once it starts to get dark I head back, emptying a trash can round the corner from my street and tipping out the contents of its bag so I have something to fill with Art Rivera's inheritance later that night. The plan for the evening is to sit at my window and watch the street below for that creep Rivera to leave Pleasance Heights, since my knack has told me his ma will be on her own when she checks out.

So I step out of the blasting wind and through the 'lobby' of my crummy hotel. I'm knocking back a handful of painkillers when Drunken-Stupor Man perks up. That's unusual.

'Uh, kid,' he hiccups, 'hold up.'

Acute pancreatitis! Acute pancreatitis! Acute pancreatitis!

'Your daddy was here.'

I stop dead.

'What did you say?'

'Sent him on up. Said he had clean clothes to drop off for ya.' He burps and looks down at that hobo's piss-stained tweed overcoat I'm still wearing. 'Thought you could use it.'

I spot a key sitting out on his desk with my room number written on its tag, having been used then left.

Crappers.

I turn and bolt up the stairs faster than I ever knew I could move. I know what I'm going to find before I crash through the door into my rancid little room.

The mattress is upturned, my cash gone.

What I didn't expect is written in the red ink of Livvy's pen over my penciled calendar on the wall:

MISS YOU LITTLE LEECH

I scramble to the window and look over at the Rivera apartment.

Drapes are closed.

So I guess he must have spotted me watching his window from my room, then started watching me himself, and waited for the best time to come over and trash my place to teach me a lesson. The cash must have been a bonus for him. He was watching all this time.

Anyways, it's dark out. The New Year bells are approaching. If there's anything to my knack at all then Mrs. Rivera must now either be dead or due to die soon. I grab the empty trash bag and head for the door, before stopping at the corner desk. I slowly open its drawer and pull out my ma's kitchen knife, its edge still marked with dried blood. I hold it to my nose and breathe in whatever's left of my sweet ma.

Every dime of Mrs. Rivera's savings. The cash he stole from under my mattress. It's all ours, Livvy.

Whether or not the old crone's croaked yet, it's all ours.

No more Crighton the coward.

***

So by now the streets are packed. There's still the odd protester do-gooder, but mostly it's people out to see in the New Year and get wrecked and fight and fall asleep in the gutter. God, I couldn't wait to get out of this city.

Anyways, the noise of the crowds is overwhelming. So much death, meant only for me to hear. Every brain cell is bloating with death, my skull wrestling to keep it all from exploding out of my head. I push on across the street through the incessantly driving snow, trash bag in hand. I feel the knife through the plastic. I find my way round the rear of Pleasance Heights, shimmy the back door lock, creep in, and make my way up the dark staircase. Down the landing I spy our old apartment door. My hands beg to knead Livvy's feet one final time, to be in our safe place together again behind our closed door, but that can't be. The only thing I can do for her now lies behind another door.

So there I am, outside the Rivera apartment, staring at the stupid festive wreath on the front door. I can hear Bing Crosby dream of his lousy white Christmas from inside. For once it's not accompanied by the smell of enchiladas or tacos or chorizos, although the very thought makes my stomach moan. I take a bite of butter. The sound of Mr. Rivera clattering around inside is also absent.

This is my moment. I try the door.

Locked.

The window above is open as usual, just as I'd hoped. I step quietly over to the storeroom, which I know is always unlocked, and retrieve the stepladder. After setting it up outside the Rivera apartment door, I climb carefully up to the window and lower myself down into the hallway as quietly as I can. Not that I need to be quiet. She'll have expired by this point. Nevertheless, I take the knife out of the trash bag. Can't be too careful. I sniff the blade then proceed silently down the corridor towards the living room.

I freeze at the sight before me.

In some ways the room is a carbon copy of our old place. The furniture is arranged the same, the carpeting and wallpaper are identical, and even the roof access is in the same spot. Except in place of our family photographs and memorabilia from Livvy's stage years filling every inch of wall, there's something else. Lots of something else.

Christmas decorations.

There's so much of the junk that it would have made our apartment look positively minimal in decor. Amongst the trinkets and baubles and other random festive knick-knacks covering every surface are garlands, reindeer-shaped bunting, and long streams of tinsel pinned across the walls. There's framed paintings of nativity scenes, carol singers, and frozen ponds filled with grinning ice skaters, the frames of which are laden with so much dust it seems entirely plausible this place's festivities are a year-round installment.

And of course, in the corner by the television set, the tree. Whether from the weight of its hundred thousand decorations, or simply from its height exceeding that of the room, the thing slumps over with a hunch not unlike Mrs. Rivera's.

But despite this Yuletide insanity, the apartment is similar enough to the home Livvy and I shared to throw up all the old memories of our life together, which ends up making me feel a bit lightheaded and dizzy. Guess I nearly black out at this point, what with all those memories flooding back, but I keep it together. There's no time to hang around. I have to move fast.

Before I know it I'm looking down at old Mrs. Rivera's stiff face, her mouth agape, just like all the others. They all look like fish gulping for water in their last moments, and she's no exception. She is pretty though, and there's something about that curly white hair tumbling over her hunched shoulders. Nice looking lady, just how I imagine

Livvy would have looked in her old age – if she'd grown her hair again, that is.

Anyways, there's no need for the knife. I drop it back into the trash bag and remove the needle from her record. Bing takes five. I'm still feeling dizzy, but I fight it. Now is not the time for a blackout. I turn to begin my search of the apartment.

And there he is, standing watching me in the opened front door at the end of the hall, covered in snow.

Mr. Rivera.

'Come for your money, leech?' he calls through.

Brain hemorr— No. I'm beginning to think the brain hemorrhage fourteen years from now isn't good enough for this guy. I finally got out there on my own, found some independence for myself (through pretty weird circumstances, I'll admit), and on top of everything he's already done he waltzes into my hotel room and takes all my hard-earned cash? No, there's no way fourteen years is soon enough for Mr. Rivera.

'You know, Crighton, you might have been able to fool your mother, but you never fooled me. Always creeping out of the building, leaving for hours at a time to go God only knows where…you're a weirdo, probably capable of anything, just a—'

His smile begins to waver as he studies my face. The words stop. He moves through the hallway and into the living room, watching the blood rush to my face. I'm studying his latest jumper, trying to figure out what its garish text says under its covering of snow, until my eyes flick momentarily to his dead ma. His widen. He rushes around the front of Mrs. Rivera, shoving me out of the way, then drops to his knees.

'*Mama?*' he pleads, holding her by the shoulders.

'What's he done to you, Mama?'

He lifts her off the couch and lowers her to the ground, then checks for a pulse. I can tell from his face there is none. Regardless, he begins pumping her chest and blowing into her mouth. Having lost my own ma, I can't help but feel a twang of sympathy for the man. We both know she's gone, that there's nothing left to do, but he persists. Eventually the pumping slows as he starts to give up. He stops, then sort of slumps over her as if he's ran out of batteries. At first I think his shoulders are jerking up and down from crying, but it soon becomes clear it's from a quickening of breath. Faster and faster those shoulders jerk until he seems ready to explode.

Then he does.

'Mr. Rivera, I didn't do it. She was like that when I—'

I don't get a chance to finish before he pounces. There's no order to the limbs and hands and feet that fly towards me, just a flailing mass of body parts that hit me like a train. I manage to get my hands on him so I can try to restrain him, all the while screaming that I hadn't killed 'Mama', but it's no use. There's no reasoning with him. He doesn't even hear my words.

We fall back into a cabinet covered in yellow, red, and green strings of lametta, knocking over a china vase in the process. It smashes on the ground, sending the cash savings of countless deceased old crones flying everywhere – *my* cash. That's the reminder I need, the reminder of who this creep is. I cease my attempts to reason with him. Maybe I begin *wanting* him to think I killed his ma. Let him hate me, like I hate him.

We claw at each other like bears in a scrap. He slams his fist into my nose, spraying blood across Mrs. Rivera's baby blue bathrobe. I launch my whole bulk at him, sending us tumbling back into the carpet of broken china and blood-stained bills. We eventually lock up like two broken cogs, our equal strength allowing neither of us to give nor take any ground. I glance down at his woolly jumper. Its covering of snow has now melted. I BELIEVE IN PEACE, its text reads through a frame of knitted holly and tinsel. And all the while his eyes, pits of fiery hate, scream their loathing into my face.

I glance over his shoulder to the open front door and see a gathering of tenants from around the building standing there, watching open-mouthed. One of them, Neighbor #3—

Toaster electrocution!

—announces something about calling the cops, then runs off down the corridor. That's not good. If I don't get the cash – Mrs. Rivera's stash or my collections he stole – I have no way out of this city. It's not like I could keep collecting if the cops answer Neighbor #3's call and get involved. Even if they didn't figure out what I'd been doing, everything I'd been stealing, they'd have me on file and— What am I talking about?! Of course they'd figure out what I'd been doing. I'd be screwed.

No, I need the money. In my confusion and rage I imagine being stuck in this town forever with people like Mr. Rivera. I feel the anger rising in my stomach.

'This city's full of nutjob delinquents like you. You're just another mad scumbag, another *coon* scumbag. Just like your dear dead daddy.'

The words float from Art's mouth, detached. For a moment I see them just like the stupid snow outside, something lousy and dumb, but for which no one is responsible. Just nature playing out. Then it clicks that they're *his* words, deliberate and despicable.

To hell with his brain hemorrhage.

Some new reserve of strength opens up before me and I throw him onto the bloodied bills, clamping my hands around his throat. What I feel in that moment, throttling him, is a sensation somehow not unfamiliar. That feeling of power, control, *freedom*. I recognized it. Anyways, choking the life out of that bonehead was ecstasy, but it didn't last. He locks his arms around me and rolls us over, practically on top of poor old Mrs. Rivera, and sits with all his weight on me.

And that's when it happens.

Never again would I see the death in a living face. Did I die? No, not yet. But as Mr. Rivera's thumbs press through my eye sockets, as I feel that insurmountable pressure growing in the ocular orifices of my skull, I know the last thing I'll ever see has already flashed before me. It was there, turned to a blur, then black. Was it the sweet, delicate features of my Livvy?

No. It was the sneering face of that goateed rodent, Rivera.

I lash out all around, my body's last strains of desperate survival reaching for some scrap of hope in this new pitch-black world. Then I find it. My thrashing hand finds the trash bag, then the knife, then Mr. Rivera. I don't know what part of him the blade meets. My effort isn't lethal, but it's enough to get him off me.

I leap to my feet, the pain in my eye sockets throbbing in depths I didn't know existed. I press my forearm against where my eyes should have been as I slash the knife in the direction of my enemy's moaning and groaning. As I do so, I back away to where I was sure I'd seen the roof access.

Somehow I make it up the ladder and out the hatch onto the rooftop. Why? Where was there to go but down?

I'd like to say I clambered up onto the roof so I could swan dive out of this life on my own terms, before Mr. Rivera got me or the cops finally showed up or anything else, but that would be lying. In truth, the new blackness brought on by the pulverizing of my eyes didn't seem so bad. It reminded me of those black skies Livvy and I would spend our nights staring up at, talking endlessly of everything and nothing. And that's why I went up there. I think I knew these were my final moments, and all I wanted to do was get to the only place I still felt my Livvy.

So, gripping the knife, I make my way carefully along the rooftop in the direction of our old spot, where we'd lie on our deckchairs. The streets below roar with New Year celebrations, every measure of that chaos screaming into my mind death upon death upon death.

Diabetes!

Homicide!

Stroke!

The faces are gone, but the voices remain. The explosions of death in my mind are still tormenting me.

I make my way along the rooftop, groping for the deckchairs. I can't find them – maybe they've been removed – so I drop the knife and press bloodied fingers into my ears instead, trying to block out the death swarming up from the streets. I hold my face up to the snowfall, the agony of my wounds cooling under the falling flakes. Maybe the snow isn't so bad after all. The blackness that's replaced my vision is so absolute that I keep wondering if I've blacked out and I'm just staring into unconsciousness, but no. I'm still here. That emptiness, though. It's so devoid, so painfully devoid of the stars we'd gazed into night after night. How I'd love to see them one last time. Anyways, I try to enjoy these final moments, but the death from below does not relent.

Kidney disease!

Malaria!

Sepsis!

Sepsis.

Livvy.

'The chairs are gone, you fucking psycho.' I take my fingers out of my ears. 'They're gone, just like your whore of a mother.'

I turn to face the voice calling from back along the rooftops by the access.

'She was even more of a freak than you, my chubby little leech.'

I scream something back at him, but I can't remember what. I think I used words I don't usually use. Maybe told him to shove *something* up *somewhere*, but it did no good. He had one last agony to inflict upon me.

'You know about Olivia's...what do they call it...self-harming. Correct?' His voice raises. 'I can't really blame her with a son like you.'

Guess I screamed something else. Didn't make a difference.

'I got a fright when she took her clothes off the first time and I saw those arms,' he calls, ignoring my cries. I hear him trudging towards me through the snow. 'You should have seen them, Crighton. Just *covered* in scars. Of course, she was determined it wouldn't be a regular thing like before. Well, every time I took her down that landing to fulfil the conditions of our arrangement, and once I'd had my way with her, she'd be banging on about how much she missed it, how much it helped with her guilt. Well, I got *sick* of hearing about it.'

The snow starts picking up, its gentle descent now the

makings of a blizzard. My ears throb with the pain of both the earache and Mr. Rivera's words. He suddenly bellows through the gale.

'I TOLD HER SHE *SHOULD*, CRIGHTON. I told her a little wouldn't hurt, and she got *RIGHT* back into it! Do you understand? You may have killed my mama, but I got your Olivia cutting again, and she *paid* for it.'

I drop to my knees and cover my flaming ears, but his yelling still makes its way into my head. My eyes are gone, and with them his face, but his words are a torment unlike anything.

'You know why she did it, Crighton? You know what this guilt was that she was covering up with scars? *You*, my boy. Guilty for *you* not having a father, guilty for *you* not having a life of your own, guilty for *you* not doing anything with yourself; for *YOUR* future, for *YOU* not working, for *YOU* not becoming anything. For you, *you*, *YOU*.' His voice pours over me, burning like molten lead. 'GUILTY. GUILTY. GUILTY. And you think she would have tortured herself like that if you'd been out there being a *man*, taking care of her like I took care of *my* mama?' He grabs my shoulders. 'It was all Olivia's marching around the city for you that tore up her feet, but she got hooked on the pain. Told me every step eased her guilt. She wanted her feet to get worse. She *wanted* it. Do you understand? She wanted it so bad she started cutting the wounds in her feet, making them worse. She knew she should stop, but I told her it was okay. She was more fun when she'd had her fix, you see. She could relax and fulfil our arrangement more...*enthusiastically*. The wound that killed her, the gash that led to her blood poisoning: I put the knife in her hand, Crighton.' He shakes me. 'That *very* knife at your *FEET*.' He kneels down and whispers into my ear. 'But she did it all because of you…*mon chéri.*'

I reach down and grab the knife, then thrust the blade into his words. Now that my world is black, his voice and every voice from the streets below throw up another blizzard besides that of the snow, a blizzard inside my head of death and suffering and anguish. I can't take it much longer, this I know.

And so I throw every part of me into him. I imagine myself as a storm, a hurricane a zillion times the power of him or the New Year revelers below or anything else in this crummy city. I drive the knife towards him.

He grabs my wrists. My feet are kicked out from under me.

I crumble to the ground, the pathetic, fat little kid I've always been. I manage to keep hold of the knife, but with my wrists pinned down either side of my head there's nothing I can do. And all the while those damned voices and cheers and screams and laughter spiral up from the swarms of vermin below.

Cervical cancer!

'It's *okay*, Olivia,' he jeers through the roaring of the crowds. 'It's just a little scratch!'

Child birth!

'Olivia, my dear…'

Skiing accident!

'…it's just…'

Firework to the face!

'…A SCRATCH!'

I don't really know how to tell you what I did next. If you've gotten this far you probably already know I can get pretty kooky. If not, this should do it. My mind stared through demolished eye sockets, a void so complete. The emptiness of my vision was accompanied by the whirlwind of death from the streets below. Midnight must have finally hit because the sound of the New Year crowds renewed, fresh waves of death rolling over me, mixing with the burning earache. And all the while Mr. Rivera's words hammered away in my brain.

'Just a scratch! *Just a scratch! JUST A SCRATCH!'*

It had to end.

I poured all my remaining strength into my pinned hand holding the knife, forcing its steely tip towards my ear. Maybe you know what I'm going to tell you, what came next, although you might not believe it. Mr. Rivera must have seen my intentions. He relaxed his grip just enough to let me do what he saw I needed to do.

I pushed the tip of the knife into my ear.

A fresh agony emerged from the darkness and overrode the torment of my mutilated eyes. It drowned everything out: his taunting, the raging earache, the death from below, the New Year bells, the thrashing gale, the sound of my own pathetic whimpering and moaning – all of it. Whether from some untapped reservoir of strength, or from Mr. Rivera relaxing his hold over me, I yanked my hands from his grasp and laid into the other ear, finally cutting that damned knack right out of my head.

I gouged the voices from my ears until, at long last, there was silence.

***

And then I died.

Or at least that's the last thing I remember before I died.

I'd be lying if I said I wasn't a little curious as to how it happened. Did Mr. Rivera get a turn at cutting me up with

71

the knife? Did I fall off the edge of the roof? Maybe both. Guess I might have finally blacked out and just bled to death. However it happened, there's one thing I know for sure: they'll all have thought I killed Mrs. Rivera. Not that I care. There was only ever one person I wanted to make happy, and you know who that was.

I don't know who you are, why you gave me this pen and paper, or where I am. It's certainly not Heaven, but it's not quite Hell, either. Guess I'll go with Purgatory, or some other brand of afterlife no one knows about except the folks that wind up here.

I still have a body. I still breathe, itch, feel the cold, feel the heat, all that stuff. You help me pee, and you even feed me (you never give me enough butter, by the way). As for the pain, I'm getting used to it. The two bloody holes where my eyes used to be and the gouged craters on the sides of my head are far preferable to what I put up with before, what my knack was becoming. Never again will my head be filled with that endless death from the faces and voices all around me. The onslaught is over. I live in darkness now, and crappers, you'd better believe it's great.

Of course my main torment, and one that will never leave me, is my unresolved hatred for the man named Art Rivera. I try not to spend too long lingering on thoughts of him, but I do find myself slipping into fantasies of his approaching brain hemorrhage. Wishful prayers materialize randomly in my head, prayers that his eventual death will cause him even an iota of the pain I've endured. The thought of it tearing his mind apart is a joy I'll cling onto forever.

Suppose I'll never write that knockout play I always dreamt of. No matter, I think I realize now that the play was never important. I wish I'd spent less time slaving away over my writing and more time appreciating my ma, maybe becoming a proper man and caring for her. I guess in some ways the rat was right. Still, through everything I've written here, I know I did the best I knew how to do. I went through more than most people will ever face. Come to think of it, I'm not so sure I feel much like a coward anymore.

Maybe this odd little thing I've scribbled down for you will have to be my *Le Testament*. It's certainly my last one, anyways. Maybe Mr. Rivera was also right about Livvy suffering so much because of me, but I've managed to convince myself that she knew I did my best. I have a feeling she'd even be proud with what I endured after she died, as well as what I tried to do for her. And you know what else? I reckon she's probably sitting right here with me.

Maybe this is Heaven after all.

HADDEN OAK PSYCHIATRIC CENTER
PATIENT EVALUATION FORM 17(B)

COMPLETED BY:
   Dr. Frida McLaughlin

REFERRAL:
   Morcaster City Psychiatric Review
   Board

PATIENT DETAILS:

Surname	Smythe
First name	Crighton
Middle name/s	Maupassant
Date of transfer	07/18/73
Diagnosis	N/A

NOTES:

The preceding text is a transcription of
the handwritten testimony given by
Crighton Maupassant Smythe (patient #429).

I (Dr. Frida McLaughlin) personally worked
on Mr. Smythe's case in Morcaster City,
and requested my own transfer to Hadden
Oak so I could follow his progress and
attempt to contribute to his treatment and
potential recovery. I am fully aware of
the regulations surrounding patients being
given writing implements of any kind, such
as the one I gave to Mr. Smythe to write
this testimony. Nevertheless, I had reason
to believe that (if his lack of sight
allowed him) the patient would open up
when given the chance to once more put pen
to paper. I am willing to accept the
consequences of my actions. The preceding

testimony makes up only a small part of Mr. Smythe's psychiatric dossier, but I believe it will prove the most significant contributor to his eventual diagnosis, treatment, and care.

As highlighted elsewhere in these reports, ocular and auricular injury-related sensory deprivation goes some way in explaining Mr. Smythe's unresponsiveness during detainment and questioning. However, I believe extreme trauma-induced stress paired with some kind of dissociative disorder may contribute even more, with the retriggering of his mother's psychotic episodes via sepsis-associated encephalopathy (resulting in a particularly traumatic incident involving Mrs. Smythe, as described herein) no doubt playing a significant role in the escalation of his violent and homicidal – albeit incognizant – behavior.

Unsurprisingly, he was deemed unfit to stand trial. I see in Mr. Smythe a confused, deluded young man, whose family has a clear history of mental illness, and whose psychiatric impairment extends beyond our current understanding. I have spent countless hours personally assessing Mr. Smythe (and countless more deciphering and transcribing his sightless scrawls) and have found no warning signs of any residual desire to cause harm to himself. It is for these reasons, amongst others, I placed the pen and paper in Crighton's hands. Due to my breach of regulations, I am aware this will probably be the last psychiatric report I write.

We may never know exactly how many died at the hands of Crighton Smythe (this written account at least tells us the figure exceeds those listed in the recovered 'client notebook', as he called it) but I believe the contents of this transcription goes far in explaining the patient's motivations and state of mind throughout the period of his homicidal activities. The blackouts he describes contribute to my theory of a psychotic dissociative disorder we may never have seen, rendering the patient oblivious to his murderous actions. This testimony will help in establishing the make-up of such a disorder, as well as of Crighton Smythe himself.

Dr. Frida McLaughlin

Gavin Gardiner's lifelong love of horror didn't manifest into his debut novel, *For Rye*, until his early thirties. Between its completion and eventual publication, he wrote this novella, several short stories, and a selection of non-fiction articles and analysis pieces. These can be found in various online publications and in print via:

www.gavingardinerhorror.com

Before he threw himself into the writing game, Gavin dedicated much of his teen years and twenties to the pursuit of music. Although the nightmares he's since committed to the page have garnered more attention than his songs ever did, he hopes to one day return to music. The writing of horror, however, is here to stay.

He's currently working on his second novel, *Witchcraft on Rücken Ridge*, and has grand plans for the future of his unique brand of horror. He very much hopes you'll join him for the ride, and consider leaving an honest Amazon review for the book you've just read, no matter how brief. Reviews are absolutely integral to the visibility of an author's work, and this visibility will help drive on the creation of further nightmares for your deranged delectation.

He lives in Glasgow, Scotland with his ever-patient girlfriend and ever-demanding kitten.

Connect with Gavin on the platform of your choice:
linktr.ee/GGardinerHorror

Also from Gavin Gardiner...

FOR RYE

Renata Wakefield, a traumatised novelist on the brink of suicide, is drawn back to her childhood hometown following her mother's ritualistic murder. Before long, she becomes ensnared in the mysteries of Millbury Peak as one question lies heavy:

Who killed Sylvia Wakefield?

As the answer draws nearer, as madness continues to envelope the quaint country town, Renata will come to realise that the key to all this insanity lies with one man – the world's leading writer of horror fiction. His name is Quentin C. Rye, and he will guide her to the revelation that true madness lies within.

Discovering that the darkness of her family's history runs deeper than she ever could have imagined, Renata Wakefield's eyes will finally be opened to one single, hideous truth, which will awaken a long dormant evil.

Turn the page for an exclusive extract from Gavin Gardiner's critically acclaimed and shocking debut horror novel...

1

Knives.

'Madam?'

Everywhere, knives.

'Are you all right?'

Knives in the eyes of every onlooker, each glance carving red-hot rivulets of pain through her flesh.

'You'll need your ticket.'

Everywhere, knives; everywhere, eyes.

She plunged trembling fingers into her worn leather satchel. *Damned thing must be in here somewhere*, she thought in the moment before her bag fell to the concrete flooring of Stonemount Central. The ticket collector's eyes converged with her own upon the sacred square slip, tangled amongst the only other occupant of the fallen satchel: a coil of hemp rope.

They stared at the noose.

The moment lingered like an uninvited ghost. The woman fumbled the rope back into the bag and sprang to her feet, before shoving the ticket into his hand, grabbing her small suitcase, and lurching into the knives, into the eyes.

The crowd knocked past. A flickering departure board passed overhead as she wrestled through the profusion of faces, every eye a poised blade. The stare of a school uniformed boy trailing by his mother's hand fell upon her, boiling water on skin. She jerked back, failing to contain a shriek of pain. Swarms of eyes turned to look. The boy sniggered. She pulled her duffle coat tight and pushed onward.

The hordes obscured her line of sight; the exit had to be nearby, somewhere through these eyes of agony. She prayed the detective – no, no more praying – she *hoped* the detective would be waiting outside to drive her, as promised. One last leg of the journey, out of the city of Stonemount and back to her childhood home after nearly thirty years.

Back to Millbury Peak.

She stumbled into a standing suitcase. The eyes of its owner tore at her flesh as she knocked it over and scrambled to regain her footing. She dared not look back as she struggled away, silently cursing the letter to have dragged her back to this unfamiliar hell, to have ripped her from her haven hundreds of miles away, forcing her to trade her cottage on that bleak, storm-soaked island for a town she hadn't called home for decades. Not since the accident. Not since the seventeen-year-old had found in white corridors and hospital beds a new home. But this wasn't about her. No, this was about an elderly lady, butchered. She was returning to Millbury Peak for her mother, her sweet, slaughtered mother. She slipped a hand into the leather satchel—

It would have held.

—and felt the coarse hemp of the noose against her fingers. She shouldn't be here. She would have been gone—

It was strong, solid.

—had it not been for the detective's letter. Gone to nowhere, forever. No more knives, no more eyes. She'd planned to be gone. She should have been gone.

The beam would have held. It was strong, solid. It would

have held.

With desperation she glanced around, the exit to this damned train station still hidden from view. She spotted a gap in the bodies. Through this gap she spied solitude: the open door of a bookshop, deserted. She went to it.

The woman lunged through the door, the teenage cashier behind the counter glancing up momentarily before returning to her magazine, uninterested. She shuffled between the rows of bookcases and backed into an obscured, shadowy corner to calm herself. She passed her hands over her bunned hair, quickly checking the headful of clips and clasps before once again reaching into the satchel. She closed her eyes as she ran her fingers over the coiled noose. The knives, the eyes, the faces. Soon, they'd all be gone.

Soon, she'd be gone.

She was turning to leave the bookshop when a thought came to her. A gift for her father, how nice.

just bruises

After all, they were separated by decades from their last meeting. Yes, she'd see if she could pick up one of her novels for him. How lovely, how *nice*.

My love, they're just bruises. He would never hurt us, not really.

She was tiptoeing through the bookcases searching for the romance section when, upon turning a corner, she found herself in the midst of a towering dark figure. She reeled back, before realising the figure was a cardboard cut-out. The blood-red shelving of its book display fanned around the figure, macabre imagery making it obvious as to which genre it subscribed. The man depicted in the life-size cut-out wore a dark turtleneck and tweed blazer, an expression of calculated theatricality staring through thick horn-rimmed glasses. The sign above read:

HORROR HAS A NAME:
QUENTIN C. RYE
CHOOSE YOUR NIGHTMARE – IF YOU DARE

The display's centrepiece was a pseudo-altar upon which sat the author's latest release, a hardback titled *Midnight Oil.* She was turning from the display when her eye caught a thin volume squeezed between spines of increasingly doom-laden type, many screaming the words *NOW A MAJOR MOTION PICTURE.* The novel calling to her had only two words trailing its spine, two words that seemed to speak to a place buried deep within her. She reached for the book.

Its cover depicted a woman standing in the middle of a road, an emerald green dress flowing behind her in the fog. This road was empty but for one vehicle: a rust-coated pickup truck from which flames billowed, flying in its wake like tin cans from a wedding car. It tore towards the mysterious woman, who stood fearless in the face of the hurling metal. *Horror Highway*, the title read.

Suddenly, blinding pain.

The paperback dropped from her hands. Agony flashed through her head, tearing like a claw, then fell away as quickly as it had risen. She looked down to find her knuckles white around a wheel that was not there. Struggling for breath, she released her imaginary grip as a stray strand of hair floated into her vision. In a panic, she picked a fresh kirby grip from the handful in her duffle pocket and fastened it amongst the mass already intricately fixed. A loose strand meant something out of place. Something out of place meant disorder. Disorder meant disaster. She closed her eyes and thought of those long white corridors, sterile and simple, everything in its place. Her breathing settled. She'd never really left hospital, or maybe hospital had never left her. She slowly opened her eyes and turned from the Quentin C. Rye display. Find the book – it'll be *nice* – then get out of here.

...he would never hurt us.

ROMANCE read faded lettering above a shelving unit at the far end. She stepped towards the unassuming section and traced a finger along the alphabetised volumes towards W.

The cashier scanned the book's barcode, offering the woman not a glimmer of recognition.

Just how she liked it.

'From one writer to another, being spotted with your own book ain't the most flattering of images.'

The voice materialised from many. She stood at the pick-up spot on the street outside the station, hesitating before looking around to the source of the voice. She glanced instead at the book in her hands as if to remind herself of whom the voice spoke:

A Love Encased
The latest in the Adelaide Addington series
Renata Wakefield

'Miss Wakefield,' the voice said with a New England twang, 'it's a pleasure. Big fan.'

She turned to find a pair of thick horn-rimmed glasses watching her, the same glasses from the Quentin C. Rye display. The same face from the Quentin C. Rye display.

Quentin C. Rye.

'My wife is anyway – ex-wife, that is.'

Her mouth refused to open. The burning pickup truck and emerald green dress filled her head.

'Didn't mean to startle you, Renata,' he said, slipping a fat leather notebook back into his blazer. He ran his fingers through slicked back hair shot with streaks of grey, then held out a hand. 'Don't mind if I call you Renata?'

So many years avoiding human interaction and it should be this American to greet her upon resurfacing? Of all people, of all eyes, why were *his* welcoming her back to the place she hadn't called home for three decades? You couldn't write it. She should know.

Renata stared at the outstretched hand.

'Your work's kinda outside my field of expertise,' he continued, twirling a pen between the fingers of his other hand, 'but I've been assured you're quite the talent.'

'I'm sorry, I—'

'Name's Quentin. The local cops asked me to help with the investigation after your Mom's…uh…' His brown frames glanced over her shoulder. 'Detective! How's it going? You guys know each other, right?'

The bulky detective stepped towards Renata, his wrinkles multiplying as he strained against the afternoon sun. 'We did a long time ago.' He smoothed his long navy raincoat, chewing on a toothpick straight from a forties noir. 'Maybe long enough for you to have forgotten. It's Hector, Detective Hector O'Connell.' He held out a hand. This one she shook, noticing its slight tremble. She risked a glance at the man. He was right: she barely remembered this greying face in front of her, but she did recognise something pained in that deep-set gaze. Not the beginnings of jaundice-yellowing looking back at her, but something else, something that stared from every mirror she'd ever gazed into. Whatever it was, it didn't stab with the same ferocity as those in the station.

She looked away.

'Your parents have been friends of mine since you were a girl, Miss Wakefield,' he rumbled, scratching his sweat-stricken bald head. 'I'm the officer who contacted you following your mother's death.' Then, lowering his voice, 'This must be a lot to take in. There'll be time to talk in the car, but know that Sylvia Wakefield was loved by everyone in Millbury Peak. We'll find her killer.'

Millbury Peak: a name both vague and clear as crystal.

'I'll follow,' said Quentin. A cigarette had replaced the pen twirling between his fingers. 'Listen, I've rented a little place on the same side of town as your dad's house—' *Little place.* The bestselling horror novelist of all-time had rented a *little place.* Renata glanced at the detective, sensing from him the same cynicism. '—so I'll be nearby if you need anything. Besides, I'll see you at the funeral tomorrow.' He pulled a crumpled packet from his blazer pocket. 'Kola Kube, Ren?'

Ren...?

'Mr Rye,' Hector began, 'I'd ask we reconvene after the service. Sensitivity is paramount at this time, and your presence at Sylvia's funeral may be unwise.'

Quentin nodded, stuffing the packet back into his pocket.

The detective took Renata's meagre suitcase and led her to a battered Vauxhall estate, as tired and worn as its owner. A carpet of empty whisky bottles, no effort having been made to hide them, clinked by her feet on the floor of the passenger side. His sweat-laden brow, trembling hands, and yellowing jaundice eyes suddenly made sense. She looked warily out at Hector.

'Small suitcase, Miss Wakefield. Travelling light?'

'I won't be around long.'

The detective smiled and gently closed the passenger door as she stuffed the book bearing her name into her satchel. Rope brushed her finger.

It would have held. The beam, it would have held.

The slam of the driver's door made her jump, causing further clinking at her feet. Hector glanced at the glass carpet. 'You should know, I just quit,' he said. 'Still to clear those out.' He pulled an old pocket watch from his tatty waistcoat – navy, like the raincoat, shirt, trousers, and every other article of clothing besides his shoes – and popped the cover's broken release switch with his toothpick. 'It made me slow, sloppy. The drink, I mean.' He gazed at the timepiece. 'Going to have to sharpen up if we want justice for your mother.' He stared at the pocket watch a moment longer, then closed the cover and slipped it back into his waistcoat. There was a roar from behind. 'These Hollywood bigshots,' he grunted, pulling himself back to reality as he wrestled the car into first gear, 'need to be seen and heard wherever they go.' Quentin's motorbike revved again. 'Never thought I'd have a Harley tailing this rust bucket.' The estate coughed to life and dragged itself from the car park.

The main road to Millbury Peak passed through twelve miles of lush English countryside beyond the city of Stonemount. Their route ran alongside the ambling River Crove, its waters losing interest intermittently to swerve off course before re-emerging from behind the oaks and sycamores. Renata gazed at the rolling fields. The air, smell, and purity of the green expanses reached to the girl she once was. Her reverie was shaken by the bellowing of Quentin's bike from behind, begging for tarmac.

Hector yanked the gearstick, a cough hacking from his throat. 'It's been decades, I understand that. If I had my way you wouldn't have been called back to Millbury Peak at all. Still, procedure's procedure, as Mr Rye kept telling me.'

'Why wouldn't you want me called back?' Renata tensed. Was she doing this right? She curled her fingers, pushing her long nails into the palms of her hands. 'I'm sorry, it's just...well, I've been away a long time, but she was still my mother.' She hesitated. 'And may I ask, Detective...why is a horror author assisting in a murder investigation?'

Hector jabbed his teeth with the toothpick. 'I was thankful for us having this time together before the funeral tomorrow, Miss Wakefield. There's things you need to hear.' He wiped the pick on the torn polyester upholstery. 'I'd like to be the one to explain the circumstances of your mother's death. I'd rather you had a reliable account to weigh any rumours against. The manner in which your mother passed was somewhat...'

His bulk shifted.

'...brutal.'

Now it was she who shifted. What 'brutal' end could Sylvia Wakefield possibly have met? Locking her eyes on the asphalt streaming beneath them, she cobbled together a mental image of her mother's face. So many memories washed away piece by piece with every passing year, but Sylvia's face remained, even after all these decades. Still, it had been so long. Why had she let the death of a virtual stranger postpone her suicide? How could her end to end all ends possibly get sidetracked by some woman she hadn't even seen in—

Promise you'll be there for him if anything happens to me.

She clenched her fists.

'As for Mr Rye,' Hector continued, 'you have every right to ask why he's here. The nature of the murder requires his presence, Miss Wakefield. You see, from the evidence available at this time, it seems the incident was…how can I put this?' He paused. 'Inspired by him.'

Renata looked up.

'Not that he's a suspect.' He rolled his shoulders as if preparing to jump the tired Vauxhall over a ravine. 'I'll be straight with you. Sylvia – that is, Mrs Wakefield – was found in the church across the fields from their house, the same house you grew up in. You remember the church, yes? The one with the clock tower?'

Clock tower. Renata's lips hinted a smile.

'Miss Wakefield, we have reason to believe whoever's responsible for your mother's death was making a statement.'

She felt like a patient being drip fed. Suddenly she knew how the crawling Harley behind them felt. She took a deep breath. 'Detective O'Connell, yes?'

'That's right, Miss Wakefield. Or Hector, whichever you'd prefer.'

She picked at her beige Aran knit. 'Detective O'Connell, I've come a long way to say goodbye to my mother and to make sure my father's in good hands.' …*my love, they're just bruises…* 'If you don't mind, I'd ask one more thing on top of the kindness you've already shown.' A strand of wool came loose. 'Be straight with me.'

For a fleeting moment she allowed his stained eyes to meet her own. She'd spent a lifetime filling pages with other people's emotions, yet, living the life of a recluse, she had little personal experience of such things. Somehow, through second-hand knowledge gained in a childhood lost to books, her writings had become like the voice-over in a nature documentary, expert narration on something she could see but never touch. That same narrator gave a name to the thing behind this man's eyes, muttering it in her ear: sadness.

'Yes, I apologise,' he said. She felt him flatten the throttle. 'Your mother was found bound on the church altar. I'm afraid…well, I'm afraid she met her end by way of…' He cleared his throat. '…fire.'

The estate lurched as if the man had just broken the news to himself.

'What are you telling me? She was burned?'

'Yes.' The detective straightened. 'The remains of Sylvia Wakefield indicate she was restrained and set alight. However, I must add there's no evidence to suggest she was conscious throughout. No gag of any kind was recovered, implying there was no need to prevent unwanted attention by way of, well, screaming. For this reason I surmise she was rendered unconscious or passed away before her…' He swallowed. '…lighting.'

Her stomach cartwheeled, then whispered: *That's your mother he's talking about, the woman who raised you. Burnt. Like a witch.*

'A note was found near her body, Miss Wakefield. It's this note that links the crime to Mr Rye. His most recent novel, a thriller by the name of *Midnight Oil*, features the strikingly similar scenario of a woman being bound and set alight upon an altar by the story's antagonist, who recites a rhyme throughout the murder. Aside from the method of execution, it is this rhyme that connects your mother's death to Mr Rye's latest work.'

'The note,' she said, eyes cemented to the grey conveyor belt passing beneath, 'my mother's killer left the rhyme at the scene?'

'Midnight, midnight…'

His voice lowered.

'…it's your turn. Clock strikes twelve…'

Her breath caught in her throat.

'…burn…'

She felt her hands tighten around that imaginary wheel.

'…burn…'

She thought of the flames.

'…burn.'

White light exploded from infinite points. She gasped as the pain tore through her head.

'Miss Wakefield, are you all right?' Hector asked. 'I said too much. You understand I just wanted you to hear the truth from a reliable source.'

The motorbike lost patience and powered past them. Renata ran her fingers over the coiled noose in her satchel, stroking the coarse hemp like a cat in her lap. Soon she'd be gone.

Her breathing levelled.

'Sorry, no. I mean, it's alright,' she stammered. 'I'm just tired from the journey.' Her hand stilled on the rope. 'Has Mr Rye been questioned?'

'Yes,' said Hector between chesty coughs. 'He cooperated fully and his alibi checks out. Poor man. Years spent writing the damned thing and some psycho comes along only to use it as a how-to manual.'

Poor man, indeed. Forges a career in torture porn, makes millions of dollars, and finally inspires someone to set fire to an old lady.

'Yes, pity,' she agreed.

'Anyway, he's devastated at the thought of his work having played a part in all this. Personally, I can't stand what he does, but I respect his efforts to put things right. He rented his…' Hector smiled. '…*little place*, and has done everything he can to help with the investigation. He's become quite the regular around Millbury Peak.'

'And my father?' Renata asked hesitantly, rubbing her wrist. 'What's he got to say about Mr Rye?'

The detective's smile faded. 'Still wears that same old vicar garb, but don't be fooled: he hasn't much positive to say about anything these days. That's another reason I wanted to explain to you the circumstances of Sylvia's – I'm sorry, Mrs Wakefield's – death. It's better coming from me than him, I think you'll come to agree.'

She already did. Her entire adult life lay between this day and the last time she'd seen her father, and yet the spectre of Thomas Wakefield had always loomed, like the ghost of a man not yet dead. Through the vast void of time, his fist forever reached.

She squeezed the noose.

…he would never hurt us.

The afternoon sun slid down a cool autumn sky as the Crove, in all its fickle meanderings, finally reconvened with the lurching Vauxhall. Quentin's Harley had long since shrank into the horizon, leaving behind only the coughs and splutters of Renata's ride. She gradually began to notice the lush fields and clear sky lighten in tone.

They were driving into a haze of mist.

Detective O'Connell switched to full beams and squinted through the windscreen. 'Not far now, Miss Wakefield,' he said. 'Just as well. Can't see a bloody thing.'

Shapes formed in the fog. Tight-knit ensembles of cross-gabled cottages and Tudor ex-priories emerged around them, triggering neural pathways long since redundant in Renata. The town was a snapshot dragged into present day, some kind of Medieval-Victorian lovechild refusing to bow to the whims of natural progression. You could practically sense from the rough brickwork and uneven cobbled roads the stubbornness with which this town opposed modernisation of any kind. It was stuck in the past, and perfectly content. The familiar forms of Renata's childhood, of this frozen town, assembled themselves as Millbury Peak unfolded in the mist.

Yet there were still gaps in her memory, scenes spliced beyond repair. There was just one thing of which she was sure: she shouldn't be here. She'd come back on the strength of a promise made when she was just a damned child. What had she been *thinking*? By now, it should all have been over.

It would have held.

'That's Mr Rye's rented house on the left.' He pointed to the Georgian manor rolling past, Quentin's Harley already leant against a side wall. 'I can tell he meant what he said. He really does want to help if you need anything.'

'I'm sure my father and I will be fine, Detective.'

Their route was leading out the east side of Millbury Peak when she spotted a stone finger pointing to the sky. Renata's eyes widened. The clock tower dominated the fog-drenched fields.

Hector glanced over. 'Must be a lot of memories.'

'Yes,' she replied.

And yet so few.

Detective O'Connell shut the engine off outside the house and heaved the handbrake with both hands. Renata pulled the book from her satchel.

'A gift?' asked Hector.

She looked at the thin paperback. 'I thought my father might like to see one of my novels.'

She felt the detective's gaze linger on the book in her hands. He scratched his stubble. 'Like I said, your parents are old friends of mine. I watched your father's health decline, his body wither, the untreated cataracts turn him blind. Thomas is not the man you knew. Although in many ways…' He glanced at the house. '…he's exactly the same.'

She stuffed the novel back into her bag and smiled at the dashboard. 'Well, I suppose I can't expect a blind man to get too excited over a book.'

'I wouldn't expect your father to get excited over anything, at least not in a good way.'

She stepped out of the passenger door onto the gravel track and stared at the towering monstrosity before her, part of her begging to get back in the car and escape to somewhere else – anywhere else. She tightened her coat.

It was a memory made real. The two-storey Victorian farmhouse had been acquired long ago by the parish for use as the town vicarage, lying conveniently close to both Millbury Peak and the church a few fields over. The struts of the wrap-around porch had seemed past their prime when Renata was a girl; now, the boards and beams resembled mildew-ridden sponges, with each of the roof's wooden shingles seemingly ready to fall to the ground with a splat.

The entrance, bay windows, veranda: all irrationally tall. The entire house looked stretched like an absurdist caricature. It dominated the fields, both a monument and a tomb. Most of all, the thing was spooky, an image of cut-and-paste cliché from a Quentin C. Rye dust jacket. *The*

Dreaded Ghost House of Doom. Or something.

Hector set down Renata's suitcase and joined her in the shadow of the house. 'I won't get in the way of your reunion,' he said. 'I'll be over to drive you to the funeral tomorrow.'

She stole a glance. *Sadness*, that expert narrator muttered again. She jerked her gaze back to the house.

'I really am sorry,' he said, voice low. 'Sylvia was an admirable woman. Mr Rye does want to assist any way he can, and I'd like to extend the same offer.'

'Thank you, Detective. I'll remember that.'

'You have a life outside of Millbury Peak, Miss Wakefield,' he whispered. 'No one will judge if you return home after the funeral.'

'I have to ensure my father's wellbeing,' said Renata, rubbing her hands. They were clammy from the journey and could do with a good wash. 'Once my brother and I have arranged care for him, I'll be leaving.'

It'll hold.

Hector's eyes dropped. 'Miss Wakefield, Noah won't be coming.'

She straightened. 'He won't be attending the service?'

'Actually, it's unclear whether your brother will be coming to Millbury Peak at all.'

She bit her lip. 'Why?'

'It was another officer who spoke with him, so I didn't get all the details. Family commitments or something.'

As excuses to dodge your own mother's funeral went, 'family commitments' was pretty rich. Like everything else in this town, her memories of Noah were vague. There was enough, however, to render this behaviour all too believable.

'I see,' she said through clenched teeth. 'Nevertheless,

I'm glad you understand I may not be staying long.'

She felt him level his gaze.

'Yes. You should leave.'

A sharp wind blew up her back. Before she could respond, the stocky detective was trudging back to his car, slamming the driver's door, and turning on the ignition. He rolled down the window.

'My regards to Mr Wakefield,' he said. Then, in a hushed tone, 'Remember, I'm here.' The rusted estate lurched into the fog. She took a deep breath.

The woman looked up at the house.

2

The house looks down at the girl.

It's like a scary face, maybe even scarier than Mr Farquharson's when she hadn't done her homework, or Mrs Crombie's when she caught her snooping around her garden, or Father's when he's having an angry day. Come to think of it, maybe not scarier than Father's. His could get SUPER scary.

But the house is like a scary face, that's for sure. There's loads of windows – not too many to count, but maybe too many to count on one hand. There's two above the porch, glaring at the little girl like a pair of eyes. The front door is a mouth, ready to gobble her up.

Anyway, it's definitely scary, and not the kind of surprise she was hoping for when Mother said Father was waiting in the car to take them somewhere. No ice cream, no penny chews, no trip to the funfair. They have popcorn at the funfair, that's what she's heard. Not that she knows much of that kind of thing, but the funfair would definitely be better than this big weird house. Besides, she might only be five-and-a-half, but she still hasn't missed the fact everything's been packed into cardboard boxes the past few weeks. She has a pretty good idea what's happening, has done for a while. She just wishes they'd spill the beans instead of treating her like…well, a five-and-a-half-year-old.

SURPRISE!

Nope, that's not what Father had said, maybe like you'd say to a five-and-a-half-year-old when you're about to take her to the circus or the beach or the funfair with the popcorn.

Instead he'd just made that gruff snorting noise that always made her nervous but also snigger a little inside 'cause that's the noise donkeys make 'cause she'd seen one in a field near school once and she even thought Father looked a bit like a big stern donkey sometimes but she wouldn't say that to his face 'cause she knew what happened when you said much of anything to his face 'cause Mother sometimes did and one time the little girl had been hit by the netball at school and it really hurt and that's probably what Father did to make the bruises appear on Mother's face – a big fat netball right on the nose. Bop.

'What do you think, love?' asks Mother with that wide encouraging smile of hers. The girl marvels at the woman's perfectly arranged hair. How does she get it so perfect? Mother squeezes her hand. The girl loves it when she squeezes her hand. 'What a big house! Think of all the places to play!'

There's a duck pond at the other house, the house called home, and she's wondering if it's coming with them. She's too scared to ask so she just pops a big smile on her face and peers around, trying to find a good pond-spot for when it gets unpacked. She says a quick little prayer in her head, asking Jesus to make sure the pond is brought along.

Father seems more interested in the big glass crucifix that usually sits on the table where other kids might have a TV but where Father has a big glass crucifix. The boxes were thrown in the back of the car like Mr Chisolm throws the squishy mats back into storage after gym class, but that big glass crucifix, oh, it sat in Father's lap the whole way here. That's what he seemed to care about most on the drive. That, and the big creepy painting of the water and the sad faces. She was pretty disappointed to see that hadn't been forgotten. If he was going to leave anything, it should've been that. Or the stupid bookcase he'd had moved in before they even got to see the place.

'Looks lovely, Mother!'

Father sets down the big glass crucifix and fiddles with the front door, his hands twitching and quivering – always twitching and quivering. Soon, the house's mouth is all wide open like a big old train tunnel. Steam trains go straight into those tunnels, they don't even slow down! The girl always found that funny 'cause she slows down whenever she goes through a door 'cause of that time she went through one too fast and BAM, there was Mother crying and Father yelling and who wants to see that? Then again, steam trains probably don't have mothers and fathers, so they don't care.

Father's red hair is all shiny in the sun. He stands next to the big old open mouth with the big glass crucifix next to him on the ground. He's looking down at her, tapping a single finger against the side of his thigh, and he wants her to go in and the little girl wishes she had a steam train 'cause right now she's not feeling too cheery about walking into that big old mouth.

Trains are brave. Maybe she'll be brave.

Maybe she'll be a train.

So Mother squeezes the little steam train's hand and off she goes, full steam ahead, 'cause that's the only direction big brave trains go.

Choo-choo!

Soon the little engine is puff-puff-puffing ahead and nope, Mother's not even holding her hand any more 'cause she's chug-chug-chugging all on her own, heading straight for that big tunnel. Trains are brave. Trains aren't afraid of some stupid old house.

The little train tears up the porch's three steps 'cause that's what trains do. Well, they don't really go up steps, but this is a special train. Three steps is nothing!

Except there's a fourth.

The little engine clips her wheel and tumbles to the ground. She bashed her whistle on the step but that's okay 'cause the whole thing's sort of funny anyway.

Oh, and she fell into the crucifix. It's in a zillion pieces now.

That's not so funny.

The gruff old donkey starts huffing and puffing and his jaw is sticking out further and further and his hands are quivering more and more and his face is turning red as a balloon and he scoops the trembling little train under one arm and off they go into that big old mouth and Mother's shouting but Father slams the house's mouth shut and it's locked now so Mother stays outside and the little steam train's on the floor and Father's staring down at her and she doesn't feel much like a brave little train no more. There he is, see? Standing over her, fists clenched.

'New house, new rules,' *he says.*

Gruff-gruff goes the donkey.

'By the Holy Book, by the sacred plight of our Lord and Saviour, that woman shall give me a son. And YOU shall bring upon yourself the solemnity of the meek.'

Bang-bang goes the door.

'Do you have any idea how long it took her to give me YOU?'

Waah-waah goes Mother.

'Lower thy head.' *He presses her face into the rough wooden floorboards.* 'Lower thy spirit before God, child, and offer upon Him a change in will, a strengthening of service.'

Flutter-flutter goes a little moth, landing next to her face.

'Change in will, strength of service. SAY IT.'

No more coal for this little engine.

'Chay-chay-change in...Father, please! You're hurting—'

'CHANGE IN WILL, STRENGTH OF SERVICE.'

'Change in…in will…'

'STRENGTH. OF. SERVICE.'

'Streh-streh…' The girl chokes on the floorboards. *'…strength of service.'*

'Yes.' Her father lowers his face to hers, his red hair not so shiny out of the sun. *'Humble thyself before His will, girl. This house shall be our salvation. Here, our family will grow. Once she finally fulfils her function, once she gives me my son, he shall grow into a man under this blessed roof.'*

His eyes cut into her.

'And YOU, my child…'

Like knives.

'…shall learn your place amongst the meek.'

Why are they like knives?!

'Now, get up. But forever keep your head to the ground. Find your place amongst the meek, girl, where you belong.' He raises a twitching, quivering hand, its fingers slowly clenching.

'Tell me you see, Renata.'

Choo-choo goes the fist.

Some
truths
are best
left
buried...

FOR
RYE

GAVIN GARDINER